My Angel 2

By Michael Conliffe

Publisher's Note

Any similarities between any characters and situations in this book to any individuals, living or dead, or actual places and situations are purely coincidental.

My Angel 2

By Michael Conliffe

CHAPTER 1

Nathan had been standing outside Tia's house for a good hour waiting on Tia to put Mioshi on some decent clothes and get her hair together. She had been with Tia's cousin Taylor all morning looking like an orphan child. Tia claimed that Taylor had left with Mioshi before she woke up. Taylor argued that Tia was the one rushing them out of the house before they could even clean their face good.

By the time Nathan got back to the car with Mioshi Myangel was no longer in the mood for the outing. They had left Myangel's place over three hours ago expecting to pick up Mioshi and continue on their way. Things didn't go as planned. They ended up going to grab a bite to eat, getting the car washed and taking the boys for fresh haircuts. Myangel had argued that it made no sense when they just had their haircut three days ago. Nathan said it wouldn't hurt. He knew it wouldn't be long before Myangel got perturbed about the way the morning was starting off. She hadn't been too thrilled about Nathan's affair and no more thrilled about the child he and his mistress created. This was their first outing with Myangel and Mioshi since the divorce was finalized. Myangel had surprised him by agreeing to go out with them. Of course the kids sealed the deal by telling her how much they would love for her to come along.

"I think I've had enough action for the day. Since we're so close, can you drop me back off at the house please?"

"Aww come on now, we all here now."

"See daddy, I told you Mommy was going to get tired" Semaja told him from the backseat.

"Well, we have been out for a long time. Mommy needs to rest and so does the baby" Gerrard told them.

"Thanks babies." Myangel couldn't help but smile at how observant and smart her kids are. "Maybe I can come along on another trip at some other time."

Nathan wanted to put up a fuss about Myangel changing her mind but he didn't want to push his luck. He knew she had every right not to go after all the drama with Tia.

Since he'd left Tia's she'd text him at least twenty times with questions and demands.

'Why did you bring her?' Her, meaning Myangel. 'If I'd have known she was going Mioshi could have stayed at home. Don't let that bitch touch my baby. When you bring Mioshi back tonight we need to talk. Bring her back tonight.'

He ignored all the text while trying to strike up a conversation with Myangel.

"What you gone do when you get home?"

"Do some work, some writing and relaxing and some nasty sleeping."

"We should be back no later than 9-9:30"

"That's cool. Semaj's inhaler is in his Nike bag. Make sure he puts it in his pocket. Make sure Semaja doesn't have anything with peanuts in it."

"Anything else Ma?"

"Yeah, keep an eye on my babies" she said to Nathan. To the kids she said, "Y'all keep an eye on each other."

"Yes ma'am" they responded.

When Nathan brought the kids home later that night they were all worn out and half sleep. Nathan helped Myangel put them to bed after washing them up a bit. She noticed that Nathan wasn't preparing to leave once the kids were all taken care of.

"Thanks for helping put them to bed. I'm glad everybody had a good time."

"Yeah you should have been with us."

"Maybe next time" she said while making her way towards the front door. *"Well alright, I'm about to get some rest. I know the kids will be up bright and early."*

"You going to Mom's for breakfast?"

"I'm glad you mentioned it because it slipped my mind but we should be there no later than 9."

"Alright, I guess you're putting me out."

"Yes sir. Good night."

"Good night."

Chapter 2

The next morning during breakfast Margaret wanted the kids to go with her to visit Salvador for a week. She asked Nathan to call Tia to find out if Mioshi could come along. They wouldn't be leaving out until the next morning. Nathan got everything squared away with Tia to have Mioshi brought to his mom's.

Later that night Margaret called Myangel to see if she'd heard from Nathan.

"I've been calling him for the last 2 hours. He won't answer."

"There's no telling where he is Mom. What's going on?"

"Tia didn't send but 3 or 4 diapers. She was supposed to bring some by but never made it. Had I known she wasn't going to show up the kids and I could have made a trip to the store earlier. They're all asleep now."

"I'll bring some. Give me a minute to get some clothes on."

"No, you don't need to be out this late."

"Mom, it's barely 11. No sense wasting time trying to call Nathan" she said while shaking her head.

Margaret tried to convince Myangel to just call Nathan to have him bring the diapers. Myangel had no doubt that Nathan was out at some club, getting ready to go or at some chick's house. She didn't realize how low her Jaguar was on gas until she got on the freeway headed to Margaret's side of town. She pulled over at a BP gas station and saw Marko standing at the pump beside her. He did a double take when he saw her but quickly recovered and instead looked like a deer caught in headlights.

"Sis, what you doing out this time of night?" He came over to her pump and took over pumping gas after she inserted her credit card.

"Getting gas" she was saying as Nathan walked out the store with Tia. They stopped a few feet away and started kissing each other.

All Marko could do was shake his head. Myangel turned her back to the scene before her.

Nathan said "I see you pulling em bro" not realizing it was Myangel standing on the other side. It took a minute for the car and stance to register completely. He quickly let go of Tia and walked over to Myangel.

"Mya, what you doing out here?"

"Taking yo baby some diapers."

"What? My babies out of diapers."

Myangel laughed while shaking her head. "Mom called, Mioshi needs diapers."

"Why she ain't call me" he asked with a dumb look on his drunk face.

As bad as Myangel wanted to go off on him, she instead held her tongue. Besides, at this point there was nothing left to say. Their divorce had been finalized for over 6 months and aside from being a father to the kids, she had no romantic interest in him. She did however have a problem with him pretending that he hadn't received not one call from his mother. She decided to leave that alone too, knowing Margaret would let him have it as soon as she saw him.

"Y'all be careful" she said before getting back into her car. Tia had started mean mugging her as soon as she saw her. Myangel didn't pay her no mind. 'Clown ass bitch' she thought to herself. Myangel has respect for those that respect her but Tia was just over the top. Nathan's actions fueled it, this Myangel was sure of. That's why she never entertained either one of them.

Myangel wasn't surprised to see Nathan in his mom's kitchen bright and early the next morning giving her a bogus explanation about losing his phone. He didn't realize Myangel was there. She gave him that look 'nigga you should be ashamed of yourself.'

Margaret wasn't buying his story no way and she told him so. While the kids were washing their hands and faces she quickly voiced her thoughts.

"You ain't learned shit, I see."

"What you talking about Ma? I told you I lost my phone."

"You ought to get tired of lying."

"What I lie about now?"

She picked up the phone and dialed his cell number. It rang from his pocket. "Whatever hoe you were with last night" she was saying as the kids started towards the kitchen.

"Come on babies, let's go watch cartoons while Gran and Daddy finish breakfast" Myangel told the kids.

Nathan assumed Myangel had told Margaret about seeing him with Tia last night and in turn told off on himself. Myangel increased the volume on the TV as Margaret really lit into him. She had a hard time holding her laugh in. Her cell started to ring. Dante' was calling.

"Hey boo"

"Don't come with that hey boo shit. What's up with you? When am I gone see you?"

"Told you I've been busy with the kids."

"I could come there or they could have come here. I've been hearing these same tired ass excuses for months now. What's the real deal?"

Just then Nathan came into the living area talking loud for whoever was on the other end of Myangel's phone to hear him.

"Oh yeah, you still on that shit huh? It's not even 8 o'clock and this nigga at the crib. No wonder you ain't getting at me" Dante' told her.

"Boy stop, Mom's taking the kids for a week and I stayed over to help her get everything in order."

"I'm not sure what you could do. You're supposed to be resting. You're doing everything but that I see. Call me when you got everything squared away."

"Ugh attitude. I'm gone see you in a few hours. We gone get that attitude in order."

"Yeah I've been hearing that for a minute now. I'll believe it when I see it."

Nathan starred at Myangel and asked "Who you all hugged up on the phone with at this time of morning?"

"None ya."

"Who is that?"

"None of ya damn business." Myangel made her way into the kitchen and said "Ma, I'm going to get going. Nathan will help with the kids. I have to find a flight."

"Where are you trying to go to?"

"To see a man about a mule."

Margaret laughed, "the meat man huh."

Myangel winked at Margaret just as Nathan and the kids come running into the kitchen.

"Hey, hey y'all know better. Stop running in here" Myangel told the kids. "Come give me hugs and kisses. Mommy will see y'all when y'all get back, okay?" She hugged and kissed the kids, including Mioshi before hugging Margaret. "Alright Mom, call me if you need anything. Y'all be careful and tell Gramps I miss him."

Semaj said "Mommy, Gramps is going to say 'Where's your mama? Why didn't she come?"

"Yep Mommy, that's what he's going to say. He said since you and daddy got too big for your britches y'all don't come around no more." Gerrard had to throw that in.

"Only on holidays" Semaja said with a shake of her head and her hands on her imaginary hips.

Nathan laughed, "You look and act just like your mama."

"Yep, I'm sho nuff cute" she said with a smile.

"You are something else lil lady" Myangel said as she kissed Semaja's forehead. "You tell Gramps I'm going to come see him soon and I won't wait until the holidays."

"Let's ride out with them now" Nathan said. "I don't have no plans. What about you?"

"I have plans" Myangel told him. "See you later Mommy and babies."

Chapter 3

"What's up" Dante' asked when Myangel called his phone.

"Where are you?"

"Where are you? Don't call me asking me no questions."

"I'm at your place. I'm hungry and as usual, you don't have food in the refrigerator."

"I'm around the block boo. You want me to grab something or do you want to eat out?"

"We can go out. I'm going to hop in the shower. I'll be ready when you get here."

"Damn Ma, look at you Dante' said as he hugged Myangel close before kissing her lips. Hands that would normally caress her face, ass and tits immediately went to her belly. The little life growing inside began to dance at his touch. Both Myangel and Dante' smiled.

"I missed you" she told him as he stood back looking her over with admiration. She blushed, Dante' still had that effect on her to this day.

"I missed you too. I'm really not feeling this long distance shit. Every day it's getting harder and harder for me," he said while still holding her in his arms.

"I know babe. I just haven't come up with a resolution that will work for everyone without further complications."

Dante' smiled as he tongued her down. "As long as it's still fresh on your mind, I'm good. A decision will have to be made soon though."

"Yes sir, I'm very much aware of that."

Myangel enjoyed time spent with Dante' as usual. Her emotions were running wild and it was becoming just as hard to be without him. She knew the time had come for the kids to spend more than just an occasional outing with Dante'. The kids no doubt adored him and knew that the two of them were dating. It was their idea not to mention this fact to their father.

Dante' kept bringing up the fact that regardless of where they decided to move to he would be around. He understood that Myangel wanted to allow the kids time to adjust to Nathan not living with them and to work through the whole divorce thing. He was patient and understanding because it was just as important to him as it was to her for Myangel to be sure of the decisions she was making. He just didn't want to be caught up in a tug of war if her heart was still with Nathan. He didn't feel that it was but had to be sure for everybody's sake.

Unbeknownst to everyone involved Myangel had already carefully considered all her options. Her heart was with Dante'. There was no confusion about where she wanted to be or who she wanted to be with. Dante' had his own law firm now. Although he had voiced his concerns on relocating since his firm was doing so well, he also readily admitted that he would do whatever needed to be done. He had no intention of losing the love of his life due to a technicality. Myangel had no intentions of losing him.

Myangel had been thinking of relocating long before the divorce came into play. She just hadn't voiced it aloud to anyone, even Dante'. Recently a lot of the kids' friends' families had started relocating due to financial issues. They moved to neighborhoods clear on the other side of town or not in town at all. This was disappointing for the kids; however it was an advantage to relocating to another state and getting a fresh start. They could always spend summers and any lengthy days out with their dad, grandma and grandpa, who would soon be moving in together or their uncles, Myangel's brothers.

She decided that now would be a good time to tell them. School would be letting out in a couple of months. Since her doctor was in Miami she wanted to have her baby delivered there as well. Dante' was in agreement with being in Miami around the delivery date and if any complications came about.

When Myangel arrived at Margaret's to pick up the kids she found out that Nathan had already picked them up.

Margaret advised Myangel that this was Nathan's attempt at trying to get Myangel on his territory. Myangel knew that this was true, however she had no intention of feeding into any more of Nathan's games. Margaret called him to tell him that the kids would be staying over the weekend because Myangel wasn't back in town yet. They both knew that he usually spent his weekends out and about. This weekend would be no different as he assured Margaret that he'd bring them back before nightfall. His plan had been to talk Myangel into another outing. He thought they were on to something on the last outing.

Tia had been dialing Nathan's number nonstop since 1 o'clock. Before he left that morning they made plans to hook up again later. Since the kids were with his Mom she didn't foresee anything causing him not to follow through. Not only wasn't he answering his phone, he wasn't responding to text messages either. Tia automatically assumed that it had something to do with Myangel. Nathan was a totally different person whenever Myangel was around.

The other night the two were kicking it real tough, really enjoying each other's company until Myangel's ass showed up at the gas station. He damn near pushed Tia away from him when he noticed her. Nathan had told Tia that Myangel wanted him back, that she wouldn't allow him to see the kids if he was with someone else. He created this big story about how he and Myangel had to be together for the kids. She believed everything he said whether it was fact or fiction.

Although he had already agreed to stay the night at her place things changed when he saw Myangel. All of a sudden he needed to go by his mom's house to make sure the kids were okay. He argued that he needed to make sure Mioshi got the diapers. When Tia called him on his bullshit he flipped it on her.

"You don't give a fuck about your own child. Mom's said she need diapers. If you would have packed the damn bag right I wouldn't have to go over there."

"Your bitch just said she was taking diapers over there. You know she did it. What you need to run in behind her for?"

"Why the fuck is you questioning me? I said I'm going to check on the kids. Shut the fuck up and let me do what I do."

Marko sat in the front seat laughing as he shook his head at the arguments between the two of them. He had been around to witness quite a few on the regular. He couldn't understand why the women put up with that shit. With Myangel he knew it was all love on both ends but with Tia and all the other side chicks there was no love, just a matter of convenience for Nathan. But shit, if they like it, I love it he told himself.

Chapter 3

"Mommy, guess who's moving to New York" Gerrard asked just before bed.

"Who baby?"

"Rashad"

Rashad is Gerrard's best friend. Those two had been inseparable for a number of years and had formed a brotherly bond. Rashad's dad had recently accepted a job offer in New York. Turns out they would be moving as soon as school let out. Gerrard was heartbroken over this news.

Myangel had planned to mention moving to the kids but she still hadn't made up her mind just how she would present the news to them. Now the moment had presented itself.

"What do you think about moving to New York?"

"Huh, We could really move there" Semaj asked.

"Ooh Mommy I told you I always wanted to live in New York," Semaja said with a huge smile.

"You're serious aren't you Mom?" Gerrard asked as he looked at her closely

She advised them all to have a seat Indian style and proceeded to tell them as much as their little ears could handle at one time.

"I think Mr. D is cool Mom and I like the idea of moving closer to Rashad now that he's moving too. But Mom I don't know about leaving Grandma and Grandpa and Daddy."

"Well Gran and I already discussed it and she and Grandpa have no problem visiting us in New York. During Spring Break and the summers or whenever school is out for a long period you guys can always spend time here with your Dad and with Grandma and Grandpa."

"Auntie Chyna said she wants to move to New York. Is she coming too?" Semaja was now playing in Myangel's hair, something she'd started doing as a baby and never tired of.

"I'm not sure what Auntie's plans are right now baby. I haven't mentioned it to her, your uncles or your Dad. I haven't even told Dante' that I made my mind up just yet."

"Well I think it's pretty cool." Gerrard kissed his Mom's cheek, happy to have some good news to share with Rashad who wasn't too happy about his relocation.

"Dad's going to have a cow when he finds out" Semaja said as she gently massaged Myangel's scalp.

They all laughed. Myangel was thankful that the kids were all in agreement with relocating. She also knew that telling them wasn't the hardest part. Telling Nathan would be, but at this point Nathan would just have to adjust in the same manner everyone else had to in the past. Nathan was still traveling and New York happens to be a spot he frequents regularly.

Myangel wasn't quite ready to deal with Nathan just yet so she waited a few days before reaching out to him. She did however tell Anthony, Chyna and Big Mike. She knew that it wouldn't be long after they found out for someone to mention it to Nathan. So she took it upon herself to contact him. She dialed Nathan's number, today would be the day any and everything was laid out on the table.

Nathan agreed to meet her for lunch at The Cheesecake Factory. He arrived late as usual but Myangel didn't mind at all. She didn't even react when Tia joined them less than ten minutes after Nathan walked in. She could tell by Nathan's facial expression that he had not invited Tia to join them. He was beyond irritated *and it showed. Instead of waiting for him to cause a scene that was indeed coming Myangel decided to be civil toward them both.*

"Hey Tia, I'm glad you could make it. Nathan wasn't sure if you'd come or not" she said with a smile.

Nathan looked at her like 'Yeah fucking right.' Tia smiled thinking she somehow had the upper hand. It took everything in Myangel not to fall out her seat laughing. Tia's presence made it easier for her to tell Nathan everything that needed to be told. They placed their orders without error. Myangel was making small talk with Tia while watching the aggravated look on Nathan's face.

"What's up man? I know you didn't call me up here for nothing."

Myangel smirked, "No Nathan, I didn't call you up here for nothing. There's no easy way to say this other than just coming out with it."

"Out with it already, damn."

"We're moving to New York."

"Who is 'we'? I know you don't think I'm letting my kids move all the way to no fucking New York."

"I clearly meant 'we" as in the kids and I. I know you didn't think I would move and leave them here."

"You got to be out your rabbit ass mind if you think my kids are going anywhere outside of Miami without me. What the fuck gave you the idea that you were even going? You have my babies he said as he nodded his head in the direction of her stomach."

"There's a possibility this might not be your baby."

"Fuck nah, you on straight bullshit. You think saying this ain't my baby gone give you a free pass? You got life and bullshit fucked up. Yo ass still ain't going no damn where. I know that's my baby. I'm the only nigga that's been hitting that and if I have it my way it's going to stay that way."

Tia looked at him like he had two heads, like she wanted to slice him up with whatever sharp object she could get. She was very well trained because all Nathan had to do was give her that look and whatever she thought about doing was quickly shut down. She still wore the frown on her face and kept giving Myangel dirty looks.

"Nathan I didn't come here to argue or debate with you. I came to let you know what's what. The decision has been made and I'm not going back on it. You travel a lot. You're away more than you're here. It's nothing for you to get to New York seeing as you're there at least 20-30% of the time which is about as much time as you spend with the kids here. It won't be any different."

Nathan looked at Myangel and laughed. "Look, I know you're still upset about how everything went down. You and Tia just need to look past all this and get over it because neither one of ya'll are going anywhere at this point. Suck that shit up and keep it moving."

Myangel watched as this cocky muthafucka sat back comfortably before enjoying his food as if the conversation had never taken place. She laughed at him, at Tia, at everything while reminding herself that what goes around comes around before asking for a to-go box and her ticket. The waiter returned quickly. Myangel was glad she had cash on her to cover the bill and the tip so she wouldn't have to sit around waiting on her credit card to come back.

Nathan sat there unfazed. Everything was a joke to him. He didn't take Myangel seriously. He didn't believe she'd ever leave Miami or him for that matter and he didn't believe that regardless of all the shit he'd done to her that she would mess around on him. He knew she talked a lot about having an open relationship in the past, she'd text a nigga every now and then and even insinuated that she'd been with another nigga but he never believed any of it. Myangel was still in love with him he believed and was only acting out after seeing Tia with him that night at the gas station. She'll be alright he told himself.

Tia couldn't wait til Myangel cleared the door before she started up with her pouting. He simply told her "Eat and then we gone head home. You looking right in that skirt. You wearing panties under that?"

Tia smiled and said "Maybe, maybe not. Guess you'll find out in a little while huh."

That's all it took with her and he knew it. He was confident that Tia wasn't going anywhere. She had proven that time and time again. She knew all about the other chicks he messed around with. A few times she had even participated in threesomes with him so he knew she would always be down for whatever. Her only real problem was Myangel. Myangel was a real threat to her. She knew Nathan didn't care about them other bitches but she'd somehow convinced herself that Nathan really cared about her and that Myangel just kept getting in the way because she had his babies. If Myangel really was moving to New York Tia would forever be grateful.

Chapter 4

Nathan tried his best to play the hard role. He took a few trips out of town only staying home for a day or two, sometimes only a few hours over the course of a month and a half. He thought that he was proving a point to Myangel by not being around to help with the kids, to go to Lamaze class or any other little thing she might need help with. In his mind he felt like she needed to get a taste of doing it all alone so she would reconsider moving to New York.

Tia had become his "go to girl." She enjoyed this title so much that she did everything in her power to meet all his needs in hopes that Myangel would one day be completely removed from the picture. Little did she know, if Myangel ever decided to take Nathan back it would be a wrap for their relationship. Any time Nathan and Tia had a disagreement about anything where Myangel was of concern Tia would throw at him "You got your nose so far up her ass and that ain't even your baby she carrying." Nathan didn't let Tia's rants faze him. He knew she was just jealous and no matter what he did, he knew she would continue to play her role to a T. She was his backup plan.

One night while hanging out at a club in Chicago Nathan was in his feelings after getting drunk off tequila shots. He was telling his crew how he planned to get Myangel back. He was bragging about not handling his responsibilities as a father as if he deserved some type of award.

Bishop told him "Nigga you wildin out."

"Hell yeah" Marko added.

"All that shit gone catch up with you. You gone learn."

"If this nigga ain't learned by now his ass will never learn" Marko said as he shook his head.

"Fuck is y'all talking about? Ain't shit to learn. Myangel belongs to me and it won't be long before she's back home where she belongs" Nathan told them.

"Oh yeah, what you gone do with Tia then" Bishop asked as he passed the blunt.

"Same thing I been doing, shit. Tia knows what's up."

"Shit, you done allowed Tia to get real damn comfortable bro. She gone pop one off on yo ass you fuck her over this time" Bishop told him seriously.

"That shit didn't even have no bullets in it. And you see where she at. She ain't going nowhere."

"This nigga got like 8 kids running around here and he still ain't trying to settle down" another dude from the crew laughed. He felt like Nathan was the man. A lot of men felt that you owned that title if you fucked a lot of women. Real men know that you were only the man if you found a real woman and stuck with her. Real men were looking for real women but they somehow always ended up with niggas like Nathan. He was nothing but a good o'l fashion hoe.

Marko, the only one in the group that was with his woman long term and fully committed tried to tell Nathan where he was messing up at with Myangel, long before Tia and her issue came into the picture. Nathan didn't want to listen. Nathan does what Nathan wants and didn't care who his actions hurt. Nathan hated to hear anybody tell him he was doing wrong. When Marko tried to school him Nathan got mad and started talking shit to him as if they hadn't been boys for years on end.

Nathan happened to be in Miami when Myangel went into labor. When Margaret called to tell him he had been lying in bed with some new chick he'd hooked up with but quickly dismissed her to head to the hospital. He walked into the labor and delivery area spotting Chyna, Anthony, Big Mike and Marko.

"What's up? Where my fam at? Where my babies?"

"Salvador took the kids to the cafeteria" Chyna told him.

"What room Mya in?"

"Can't nobody else go back there right now" Marko was telling him as he held him back.

"I'm the daddy nigga. I can go back there, shit."

Marko could tell that Nathan was high and tried to calm him down. Nathan got offended and started going off on Marko. Thinking back on Myangel telling him the baby might not be his and the night at the club and how heated things got between the two of them only added fuel to the fire. The two hadn't spoken since that night.

"Nigga you act like you fucking her. Oh is that your baby she carrying?"

"Man, go head with that bullshit. I ain't fucking Myangel. You should know better."

"Well fall back my nigga. This my woman we talking about and that's my baby."

Nathan heard the kids coming around the corner. He scooped them up happily. He hugged Salvador before saying "Alright let me go back here and check on my wife. Man I love that woman."

"Son, let me holla at you for a minute Salvador told him."

"Pop it's gone have to wait. Mya could be having the baby any minute now."

"Mommy already had the baby. It's a girl and her name is Jasara. She's so pretty Daddy." Semaja told him as she enjoyed the orange she was eating on.

"I need to go on back here so I can see my new baby girl" Nathan kept saying while asking for the room number again and again.

"Yo, what's up? Why ya'll trippen? Nobody want to tell me the room number and shit. Fucks up?"

"Bro, come on let's take a walk" Anthony was saying as Dante' came from the back with Margaret on his heels. The kids ran in their direction. Semaja went to her grandma first. The boys stopped to talk to Dante'.

"Yo who the fuck is this nigga?" Nathan asked loudly before heading in their direction.

Salvador, Marko and Anthony grabbed him. Chyna grabbed the kids. Margaret stood in between Dante' and the guys.

"Now is not the time for this. Don't do this here, not now." Margaret said with a stone cold glare in Nathan's direction.

Nathan started up anyway, cussing like a sailor. Salvador, Anthony and Marko damn near dragged him to the hospital's elevator and out the front door.

Margaret knew Nathan wasn't going to take everything in stride, no matter how ill his actions toward Myangel had been at any point in time. Myangel had tried being civil about everything. She had tried to talk to Nathan about the baby, about Dante' and about moving to New York on more than just the initial occasion. He still didn't take things seriously. He walked around like he had it all together and everything would work out in his favor. He had it in his head that Myangel wasn't going nowhere with 4 kids. No man would want a ready-made family no matter how good Myangel looked or how much of a real woman she was...this is what he had somehow told himself enough times that he believed it. While he was in denial and avoiding the issue altogether, Dante' had met and spent time with the kids, his mom and dad, Myangel's family and friends. Everyone else had made peace with the transition, the relocation and everything else, no matter how hard it seemed.

In the parking lot of the hospital Nathan didn't calm down. He couldn't, he was bothered by everything and it was finally showing. Sadly his contribution to the outcome hadn't yet registered at all. He was cussin, ready to fight and eventually had to be escorted off the premises.

Chapter 4

During Myangel's stay at the hospital Nathan couldn't bring himself to accept the reality of everything that was going on. In turn, every time he did arrive to visit he caused a scene until finally they told him the next time he came back he would be arrested. Everybody assumed Nathan wouldn't cause a scene if Dante' wasn't around. He proved them all wrong. It didn't matter whether Dante' was there or not, Nathan now had issues with everybody. He felt betrayed not only by Myangel but by the entire family. It bothered him to see his mother and Salvador, Marko, Anthony, Chyna and Big Mike all chummy with the cat. It hurt him to the core that the kids liked Dante'. It didn't matter that they still clearly acknowledged Nathan as their father.

"Look gotdammit, you need to put all your bullshit aside and go see about that baby." Margaret told Nathan a few days after Myangel was released. "You brought all this on yourself. You fucked this up. You kept fucking around like you didn't have a care in the world. Now you want to show your ass because everybody is moving on with their lives, accepting the reality you created. You didn't want to be married. You didn't want Myangel. You didn't take care of your family. Everything is YOU, YOU, YOU." Margaret was in her kitchen baking chicken enchiladas to take to Myangel's for dinner. Salvador was there and planned to make the trip along with her originally.

Nathan was so worked up and causing friction not only amongst himself and Myangel but his mother as well. Now she was clearly upset. Salvador decided to stay behind to have a man to man with Nathan. He hoped what he had to say would sink into Nathan's head very quickly. Myangel and the kids would be leaving for New York in less than 2 weeks. Nathan had already wasted too much time by trying to act unfazed by everything.

Once Margaret left Salvador fixed drinks for Nathan and himself. After the initial drink Nathan was on his own as far as drinking went. Salvador didn't have to initiate the conversation. Nathan started up on his own.

"Sal, this shit is fucked up. How the fuck she gone have the nigga up at the hospital like that? Who the fuck is that clown anyway?"

"You've been divorced for over a year and separated long before that. She moved on with her life. You can't hold that against her."

"I can't hold that against her? She was fucking cheating on me. She been fucking that nigga since back in law school. That same nigga used to text her 'I miss you' and shit."

"Son, I know all about that. I walked in on an argument you two were having once. I remember her telling you that she was very much aware of you messing around on her. She told you your shit was over the top and that you were going to have an open relationship if you didn't get things in order."

"She said all that shit but who the fuck believed it? I was already doing my thing long before she even mentioned that."

"So I guess you expected her to put up with your shit forever?"

"We were supposed to be married til death did us part, sickness and in health."

"Oh, you of all people want to quote wedding vows that you didn't honor. Come on now son."

"She didn't honor them. I just told you she been fucking that nigga for years and you want to take her side."

"I'm not taking anybody's side. I'm telling you what's real."

"What's real. What's real? So for her to cheat she just gets a pass but I cheat and all hell break loose huh? She run off and get knocked up by another nigga and now she trying to take my kids off to New York. Nah fuck that, them my kids. Fuck her. She can take her ass up there and take that bastard baby with her."

Salvador just looked at him, shook his head a few times before telling him "Son, one day you'll own up to your part in all this but right now you're making an even bigger mess of things."

Salvador grabbed his keys before telling Nathan *"I'm headed over to Myangel's. Don't bother coming tonight. Stay here and do some resting, get some sleep son."*

Nathan thought he would be leaving when Salvador rounded the block good. He hadn't paid attention to Salvador slipping his keys and phone into his pocket. Nathan had never been good with numbers and relied solely on his phone to get in contact with everybody. In his drunken state he couldn't even focus on calling anybody's number. After a few more shots of E&J he was laid out on the couch snoring like a baby. He hadn't been able to sleep the last few days. His mind was on Myangel and the kids moving to New York, to Myangel having an affair and having another man's baby. It didn't matter that Tia had his child and other women had aborted theirs upon his instruction and ability to pay. It didn't matter that he had been cheating on Myangel long before the twins were born or that she had come to him like a real woman to let him know that things were getting out of hand and she was going to be stepping out on her own if they didn't get back in order. Nathan measured Myangel's love for him by how much bullshit she allowed him to get away with. She had loved him true enough but she got tired of him taking her kindness for weakness. She got tired of his shit. She got tired of being mistreated. He didn't get that part though. He hadn't yet come to grasp with what might have really occurred. He was only concerned with the now and how it was affecting him.

He sent Myangel a text a few days later stating *'I want a blood test done immediately.'*

"Don't worry, it's not Dante's baby. We found that out the night Jasara was born. She is your child."

"I need proof that it ain't that nigga baby. I still want a blood test to make sure she's mine" he only threw that in there in hopes that it would hurt her in the same manner in which he was hurting. Myangel wasn't offended at all and didn't give him the reaction he was hoping for.

Instead she told him, *"Nathan we're at Dr. Manuel's now. They have Jasara's DNA on file. Call him up. I'm sure they wouldn't mind doing the testing for you to clear your head"* she told him sarcastically.

"I don't need to clear my head. You should be trying to clear your conscience. The fact that you even had the nigga tested means that you was fucking off on me. You weren't sure who baby it was. How you feel?"

"How I feel" Myangel laughed to herself before responding, "I feel absolutely great. In fact, I've never felt better" she laughed.

"Yeah what the fuck ever" was his last reply before calling up Dr. Manuel's office and requesting the testing.

A few days before Myangel was set to leave for New York Nathan received the test results back. Now that he was certain Jasara was his child he was even more content on arguing his point about them staying in Miami. His arguments ranged from how he needed to be with Jasara right now and how the kids needed to remain in the same schools with their friends. He argued that the kids needed to be able to see Mioshi, his mom and Sal. He argued that Dante' was going to get tired of taking care of another man's kids. He argued that things would soon fall apart between the two of them.

Chapter 5

Myangel had just stepped out the shower when the doorbell rang. Dante' and the kids had not too long ago left for the movies. She assumed they might have forgotten something and came back for it. She wrapped herself up snuggly in her robe before answering the door. Nathan stood on the other side with a smug look on his face.

"What's up he asked as he looked her over from head to toe with a smile"

"How can I help you" she asked without clearing the doorway.

"I came to see my babies."

"You should have called first."

"Why, so you could tell your faggot ass boyfriend to leave?"

Myangel's tongue grazed her top teeth a few seconds before she shook her head and closed the door in his face. She secured all the locks before walking back into her bedroom as she listened to him ring the doorbell. She clearly ignored him as she moisturized her body with Johnson & Johnson baby oil gel. She stepped into a pajama set just as Nathan started calling her phone. With the ringing of the doorbell and the phone Jasara started to whimper in the bassinet beside her bed.

"Hi Mommy's baby she said as she picked her up and relaxed with her back on the headboard. She got comfortable before raising her shirt and preparing to feed Jasara. Nathan was now throwing a tantrum at the front door. With Jasara latched on to her breast she made her way to the front door again.

"I came to see my baby. Open up the damn door."

The telephone rang again. Big Mike was calling to find out if it was okay for him to stop through because he was in the neighborhood.

"Sure bro. Nathan is at the door. Dante' and the kids went to the movies and it's just me and Jasara here" she was telling him when she heard a car door shut and Nathan asking "What's up"

She heard Big Mike say what's up before she opened the door.

"Hey" Big Mike said as he kissed Myangel's cheeks and gently patted Jasara on the back. He rushed into the bathroom to wash his hands.

"Are you going to come in or what" she asked Nathan who still stood on the outside looking at her crazy.

He slowly walked in and attempted to grab the baby, completely ignoring the fact that she was being fed underneath the blanket.

"Go wash your damn hands" she told him as she snatched away from him.

Her text message alert was going off. Dante was letting her know that they made it to the movies and was trying to find out if everything was okay with her and Jasara. She replied back Everything's fine. Nathan showed up but Big Mike's here so we're cool. His response was call me if you need me.

I'll always need you 👀 was her reply.

Myangel nursed Jasara a few minutes longer before burping her. Jasara snuggled into her chest and attempted to go back to sleep.

"Let me see her" Nathan said as he held his hands out for her.

The moment she left Myangel's chest she started to whimper. The longer Nathan held her the whimpers turned into an all out cry.

"What's wrong with her" he asked?

Myangel said "She has to get used to you." She placed Jasara's blanket across his shoulder and advised him to place her there and rub her back. He did as he was instructed all the while fussing about how he wasn't new to this. Myangel wasn't entertaining his argument and clearly ignored him while keeping a close eye on her baby.

After a good ten minutes with Nathan Jasara's cry became a wale. Nathan was irritated so he passed her off to Myangel as his cell phone rang. When he answered Tia was on the other line fussing about how he was supposed to be back by now. Big Mike reached out for Jasara. He held her in one hand as she opened her eyes without any tears and just stared at him.

"Hey lil mama" he said as he played with her fingers. The two were in their own world as Myangel sat with a smile on her face watching the two of them. Nathan ignored Tia as he too watched them with a scowl on his face.

"Look at this shit" he said as he threw his hands up.

After a few minutes Big Mike tried to give Jasara back to Nathan. Again she started to cry.

"Who's baby is that" Tia was asking before Nathan announced that he was leaving and would stop by later.

"Okay" Myangel told him, "call first."

"Whatever man" he said as he walked out the front door.

Big Mike shook his head.

"How did it go" Dante' asked after they got the kids off to bed.

"Same ol Nathan" she said with a sigh. "He showed up without calling. I would have left him out there if Big Mike hadn't showed."

"How did my baby react to him?"

"She cried, he didn't bother holding her long enough for her to get used to him so Big Mike held her until she fell off to sleep. He tried giving her back to Nathan and she started crying again."

"She needs to spend more time with him."

"Hard to do that when he ain't around."

"Ain't Myangel" he asked as he walked up on her slowly kissing her lips. "Ain't baby?"

She laughed, *"You know what I mean. He can't expect her to just bond with him off top. Hell he wasn't even around when I was carrying her."*

"Did you tell him the move date changed?"

"No, what for? That will only make him prolong coming to see her."

Chapter 6

"Yo, where the fuck you at? I'm at the door trying to see my kids." Nathan said through the phone as he stood outside Myangel's doorstep.

"Nathan, nobody told you to show up at my doorstep."

"Fuck you mean. I'm not trying to go through this shit with you right now. I want to see my kids."

"You'll see them when we get back to Miami."

"When you get back, what you mean when you get back? Where y'all at?"

"In New York."

"Alright man, whatever."

"Nate, when will you realize that things don't have to be so damn complicated? I'm not trying to keep the kids away from you. I just can't deal with all the drama you keep up on the regular."

"Here we go with this shit, look, how many times are you gone remind me that I fucked up, that all this is my fault? I get that. I'm saying though, why I gotta make appointments to see my own kids? Why I have to call you to find out my kids are all the fuck the way in New York? Why the fuck are y'all even in New York?"

"Why the fuck are you asking so many damn questions? Why does it even matter? I told you we already made plans for this week and to spend time with them before but you chose to do your own thing. We're not on your time Nate. You need to get your shit in order. I'm tired of bumping heads with you damn near every day. I'll call you when we get back." Myangel disconnected the call.

"You sure you will be alright until I get back" Dante' asked Myangel as they lay in bed the night before she heads back to Miami.

"I'll be fine. Everything is already packed and ready to be shipped. We will only be gone a few days. Will you be okay without us is the question?"

"Nah, not really. I'd feel better knowing I could get to you if something goes on."

"Something like what?"

"I don't know."

"You don't have to worry babe. I'll get the last of our affairs in order and by the time you get back the truck will be loaded and we can all fly back here together."

"Is there anything you want me to do before I get there? Anything you or the kids need?"

"No babe, everything is in order. I don't need you to do nothing but relax."

Myangel and the kids arrived at the airport before noon Sunday morning. Margaret and Nathan were there to pick them up.

"Hi babies" Margaret said as she kissed and hugged the kids before scooping Jasara up in her arms and kissing Myangel's cheek. "Hi mama"

Smiling she said "Hi mom, thank you. She was about to wear my arm out."

Nathan stood playing around with the kids as he watched his mom and Myangel make googly eyes at Jasara. She was so calm in his mother's arms. He allowed her a few more moments before reaching for her. Jasara didn't cry instantly but he didn't get very far with her before she started up. He held her until they walked out to the car. He buckled her into her car seat and made his way to the driver's side of his Denali. Myangel sat up front with him while Margaret sat in the back with the kids.

"Y'all want to go grab a bite to eat before heading home" Nathan asked Myangel.

"Yeah, that's cool. Where we going?"

"Let's go to Golden Corral."

Staying up all night the past few nights and very entertaining days had Myangel tired. Margaret wanted to get the kids for a few hours so Myangel decided to go home to catch up on some much needed rest.

Jasara was wide awake so Myangel wasn't able to get much sleep. Instead she finalized the insurance details for her shipment to New York.

4 months into their New York move Nathan seemed to be a little more understanding of things. He tried to visit as often as possible and there were never any arguments. He still refused to meet Dante' and only came around when Dante' wasn't home. He liked to pretend that they were all still one big happy family and that Dante' didn't exist.

It was the start of Thanksgiving break for the kids when he arrived in town. He called ahead to let Myangel know he would be coming through in a few days but wasn't sure of the exact date. The kids were out for break so he knew Myangel was home.

"I'm about to come through" he was saying when she picked up her phone right before another call came through on his end. "Say, let me hit you back" he said before giving her a chance to speak.

When he arrived at the house he wasn't expecting Dante' to answer the door. Myangel had called ahead to let Dante' know Nathan was on his way. She had tried calling Nathan to let him know Dante' would be there and that she was on her way but he never bothered to answer.

Nathan assumed Myangel had set him up. She had been trying to get the two to meet since before the New York move. She explained how important it was for Nathan and Dante' to at least get to know each other since they both would spend quite a bit of time around the kids.

Nathan had argued "Them my kids, what the fuck I need to get to know him for? When he decide to bounce I'm still gone be here."

Myangel said "Nathan, this ain't about you. I think it's important for the two of you to at least be on speaking terms for the sake of the kids. We live here for God's sake. You call or stop by and don't even acknowledge him."

"What I need to acknowledge him for? You fucking him. I ain't."

"Me fucking him has nothing to do with the fact that we're living in his house…"

"Nobody told you to move your happy ass to fucking New York in his house. You had your own house back home. Don't expect me to be all chummy with the nigga because you relocated to his house."

"Whatever Nate, the two of you will meet eventually. I don't expect y'all to become friends but damn, at least try to be civil."

"Where do you find civility in fucking another man's wife?"

"The same way I found civility with Tia after fucking my husband, and having his baby."

"Hell you ain't know if Jasara was mines or his so what's the fucking difference really? We both fucked off so don't try to guilt trip me into meeting the nigga. He ain't on my list of priorities."

"Wassup, say Mya here?"

"She and the kids went to the store. They should be on their way back. Come on in."

"Nah, I'm good. I'll just wait in the car" he said before walking off.

Dante' was giving Jasara a bath when he heard Myangel and the kids coming in.

"Mommy, I thought you said Daddy was here" Semaja asked as she carried a bag into the kitchen.

"Where's D" Gerrard asked.

Semaj had rushed into the back of the house to use the bathroom and heard Jasara's giggles as Dante' lifted her up out of her bath tub. "D's back here. He just finished giving Jas a bath." "D, even though Daddy's here, do we still get to go play ball later?"

"I don't know what the plans are just yet but if everything is still cool we will still go."

Myangel and the rest of the kids came to the back. The kids started talking to Dante' as he put Jasara's clothes on after rubbing her down with baby lotion and putting powder on her. Jasara wore a smile the entire time.

"Look at her" Myangel smiled, "she just loves the water." "Give her a bath and she just comes to life."

"D, where did my Daddy go" Semaja asked.

"He didn't want to come in. Said he would wait in the car."

"Mommy, can we go out there" Gerrard asked.

"Yeah baby, just make sure he's still parked out there before you open the door."

"Damn Ma, I want to sop you up with a biscuit right now" Dante' told Myangel as he lifted Jasara up in his arms while kissing her cheeks. He leaned over to Myangel and kissed her lips slowly offering up some tongue.

"Mmm" Myangel smiled when the kiss ended she allowed her teeth to graze her bottom lip. "I'm so glad you could get Thanksgiving break off."

"Yeah, me too" he said as he watched Jasara play with Myangel's face. "The first of many, I'm looking forward to it."

"Mommy, can we go with Daddy to Newnan's" Semaj asked.

"Tell your Daddy to come in."

"He doesn't want to come in. Told me to come ask you."

Myangel shook her head as she picked up the house phone and dialed Nathan's number. She wouldn't give him the satisfaction of stepping outside since he was too childish to come in. He allowed the phone to ring a minute before he answered.

"Wassup" he asked nonchalantly.

"How long do you plan to be at Newnan's?"

"Why? I ain't got no curfew with my own kids."

"Nate, I'm asking because we already made plans for later. How long do you plan to be in town?"

"I'm not sure yet. What time I need to have them back?"

"2"

"2? It's after 10 now."

Dante' said "If the kids are cool, we can just go some other time."

"But D I want to go today because I already told everybody I would be there" Semaj said as he looked from Dante' to his mom and then back to Dante' again.

Myangel knew that the kids had been excited about going to the new recreation center a few blocks away. All the kids from school would get together to play basketball, video games, gymnastics, dance class and a number of other activities. Nathan got offended by Semaj's announcement about wanting Dante' to take him somewhere instead of trying to hang out with his Daddy.

"It don't have to be no debate. We'll go and be back by 2. Tell Semaj to come on."

"Semaj, your Daddy will have y'all back here in time enough to go to the center. He's waiting for you." Into the phone she said "Nate, we'll see y'all when you get back." He disconnected the line without a response.

"Alright cool. See you later sissy" Semaj said as he kissed Jasara's cheek. "I can't wait til you're old enough to go with us."

Myangel walked to the front door and stood there until they pulled off.

"Babe, I was thinking we could have steak, mashed potatoes, corn on the cob and asparagus wrapped in bacon for dinner. What do you think about that" Myangel asked Dante'.

"Sounds like a plan, as long as I can have you for dessert. I'll cook. You're supposed to be getting some rest woman."

"I'm going to feed J and then put her down for a nap."

"Then you can feed me afterwards" he said with a wink.

Myangel fed Jasara, afterwards she wasn't ready for her nap so she sat in her rocker while Dante' prepared dinner. He told her what he was preparing for dinner and named off each ingredient he pulled out to show to her. She sat back thoroughly entertained. Myangel was enjoying a long hot bath after starting a load of laundry, folding another and straightening up a few things around the house.

By the time Dante' got all the food started Jasara was asleep. He picked her up in his arms, she stirred a little. He patted her back until she went back to sleep. Myangel was standing in the bathroom wrapped up in a towel as she braided her hair in a French twist. Dante' walked up behind her and allowed his hands to roam her body as his lips kissed and sucked at her neck.

It wasn't long before foreplay was underway and the two of them were seriously going at it. Jasara was asleep in her bassinet so the two remained in the bathroom so they wouldn't disturb her.

They were going for round two when the doorbell started to ring. It was 1:45, Nate had brought the kids back on time.

"Shit, that was good" Myangel said as she watched Dante' put his clothes back on and rush out to the front door.

"D, Daddy took us to the mall and I got you something" Semaja told him.

"Oh yeah, what did you get me" he asked as he picked her up in his arms to swing her around. In between tickles and giggles she told him she bought him the boxing gloves they saw on TV the other day.

"Yeah D, now we can go to the boxing ring to practice" Gerrard told him as he hopped on D's back.

Soon they all were wrestling in the foyer area and all over the house as they picked up pillows to throw at each other.

Myangel laughed and said "Alright now, bet nobody get hurt or else I'm gone hurt all of y'all."

The doorbell rang again. Nathan stood at the door with bags in his hand.

"Hey" Myangel said when she tried to step aside to let him in.

He passed her the bags instead and asked "Can I talk to you for a minute"

"Yeah Nate, what's up?" She stood in the doorway after sitting the bags on the foyer floor.

"What y'all got planned for tomorrow?"

"Nothing that I know of. Do you want to get the kids?"

"I wanted to take them tonight but I understand y'all already made plans. Can I pick them up tomorrow and keep them overnight?"

"J too?"

"Yeah, I want to see my baby."

"You can come in, you know."

"Nah I'm good. So what time can I come through tomorrow?"

"Whatever time works best for you. Like I said, we don't have anything planned."

"I'll be here no later than 10."

"Alright, see you then."

Nathan showed up on time and actually came in. Dante' was out helping a friend move some furniture for the moment but Nathan didn't know that.

"Why the hell you get up in the mornings looking so good" he asked Myangel when she answered the door.

"Shut up you nut, come on in here. The kids have had breakfast and their bags are packed." Myangel had a head scarf on her head, an oatmeal scrub all

over her face for cleansing and she rocked a t-shirt and sweats, barefoot. She took his comment as a joke.

As Myangel went over a list of things that could and couldn't be done as far as the kids were concerned Nathan asked "What kind of formula Jasara on?"

"Formula? My baby ain't on no formula."

"See, told you Daddy" Semaja told him.

"Thought you said you weren't breastfeeding no more because them two gave you hell."

"It's healthier for my baby and it's worth it."

"So what am I supposed to do when she gets hungry? You might as well come stay the night too."

"Yeah right" she laughed. "I made her some bottles. Shake them up real good, heat them a little and then shake them some more. Maja can help, right baby?"

"Yeah Daddy, I can help. I change diapers, feed her, give her baths and we watch the Disney Channel together sometimes so Mommy can have her "Me" time"

Myangel laughed, "Yes, mommy needs her "Me" time"

"Well y'all call me if you need anything. Mommy loves her babies" she said as she hugged and kissed each one.

"Mommy, when D gets home can you tell him to make sure he records the fight please and tell him to remember not to watch it until we get back" Gerrard said as he held on to her.

"Okay baby, I'll make sure he has everything in order. You keep an eye on your brother and sisters and help Daddy out, okay?"

"Of course Ma, I got this."

Laughing Myangel said "Hursh boy"

When Dante' arrived back home later he assumed that Nathan may not take Jasara with him. The two still hadn't bonded yet and once Dante' realized she was gone he didn't know if that was such a good idea.

"He's called a few times already but he'll be alright. The kids are there to help him and he will have to get used to her eventually."

Dante' had a blank look on his face.

"D" she called out to him. He was in his own world. She walked up on him from behind and wrapped her arms around his waist. He lived for these moments.

"Let's get out and chill for a minute" he said as he turned around and picked her up in his arms.

Nathan had been calling off and on all day concerning Jasara. Dante' was at the point where he was like "Let's just go get her."

"No D, we can't go pick her up every time she cries. He needs to learn how to handle her by himself. I don't know what he plans to do when he takes her to Miami with him for weeks on end. He better get it in now."

Myangel and Dante' were in the middle of sex when the doorbell rang around 10 that night.

"Yo, who the hell is that" he asked never missing a stroke.

"I don't know and I don't care. Just don't...don't stop. Don't stop" she kept telling him as the doorbell continued to ring. He didn't want to stop and didn't plan to until they both reached their climax. Because the doorbell hadn't stopped ringing he was forced to speed it up until they both were left breathless.

"I'll get the door" he said as he grabbed his robe.

Nathan was at the door. Myangel could now hear Jasara crying. She grabbed her robe and rushed to the front door. Nathan was already frowned up. He knew before he pulled up that there was a chance Myangel and Dante' were in bed. He also had a feeling they would be having sex, at least that's what he would be doing whether the kids were home or not. Seeing Myangel in her robe looking as if she was still in the middle of sex pissed him off. Dante' started speaking to the *kids. Jasara's cries softened as she searched for Dante's face. She reached for him. The minute she was in his arms she stopped crying altogether.*

"Mommy, Daddy couldn't get J to stop crying" Semaj said as he hugged her.

Semaja had been awakened out of her sleep so she too was a little fussy. Myangel picked her up in her arms and held her close until she calmed down. Gerrard was now standing near her holding her free hand.

Nathan didn't like the look of things. Jasara snuggled up in Dante's arms and the rest of the kids appeared to be happy to be back home. "Alright, I'm out" he said as he walked off.

Chapter 7

Myangel was standing in the kitchen along with Dante' preparing Thanksgiving dinner.

"You alright D baby, you've been quiet all morning."

"You think everybody will show up?"

"Yeah, why wouldn't they? You sure you're okay with this?"

"I'm good."

"The first of many, remember?" She walked over and looped her finger into his pants loop. She pulled him to their bedroom.

"Gerrard, keep an eye on everybody baby."

"I will Mommy. Semaj and Jasara are asleep. Maja's listening to music on her laptop."

"Alright baby."

"What we doing" Dante' asked with a smile as Myangel walked into their bedroom with her finger still in his pants loop closing the door behind her. She pushed his back up against the door, massaged his balls through his jeans before dropping to her knees and unzipping his pants. It wasn't long before she had him in her mouth. She could hear Naruto on surround sound coming from the living room. Dante' was still getting used to having sex with the kids in the house. No matter how creative the two could get with quickies it still took some coaching. At the moment he was very relaxed. There was a lot of built up tension between he and Nathan the last few days. Not only was Nathan salty about Dante's bond with the kids, he was bothered by the fact that everybody would be spending Thanksgiving at their house.

Back in October Margaret mentioned that she was hoping to not have to be in the kitchen for Thanksgiving or Christmas.

"Well Ma I don't know what we gone do cause you know I ain't getting in the kitchen and Tia can't cook."

"You're kidding, right?"

"Nah Ma, I'm so serious.

"What does Tia do?"

"What you mean?"

"You have a live in cook, nanny and a house cleaner. For what? You live in a damn condo and she don't do nothing but shop all day. Spending your money."

"We ballin ma."

"Really, is that what y'all call it these days?"

"Yep"

Margaret asked him about Thanksgiving a few more times and received the same answer. Sal mentioned going out to eat but Margaret wasn't feeling that. She later mentioned to Nathan that she would be going to Myangel's in New York.

"You gone go way to New York for Thanksgiving?"

"My family is there, why wouldn't I"

"Because I'm here and I ain't trying to be sitting around that nigga. I ain't feeling him like that. Why can't they come here?"

"You really need to quit" she laughed at him. "What difference does it make whether we go there or they come here? Dante' will still be present."

The next time the question was brought up he asked "Did you get an invite yet?"

"Of course we did. We will be leaving out in a couple of days."

"Going where?"

"To Myangel's, she and Dante' are cooking. Sal and I will be staying with them for a couple of weeks."

"A couple of weeks, what kind of shit is that?"

"Shit, what do you mean shit? My grandkids and my daughter are there."

"Yeah and your son is here."

"Son, let it go."

He phoned Myangel and asked "Yo, what kind of shit you trying to pull?"

"Nathan, not today. Don't start today."

"What you mean don't start today? You started this shit. Why you invite mom and pop over for Thanksgiving? They don't like that nigga you fucking and I don't either."

"Nathan, grow up. I invited your family too. It was mainly because the kids wanted you and Mioshi to come and your baby mama can't cook. But I don't have to remind you of that. Now, were you calling to tell me you guys are going to make it or are you just calling to get on my last nerve?"

"I'm saying though, why can't y'all just come home? I'll pay for flights and we can order something from Selah's. I'll even let your boyfriend stay at the house."

"Nathan, you and the family are welcome if you care to join us here at our home in New York. Everyone else has already confirmed. I need to know in advance so that I can make sure I get enough food."

"Man, I'm for real. Y'all better figure something else out.

He put up this same fuss to everybody that mentioned it to him. After all this time he still tried to make himself out to be the victim.

Dante' was releasing just as the doorbell rang. "Right on time" Myangel smiled. "You get cleaned up. I'll get the door."

Margaret and Sal were the first to arrive. Myangel had advised everyone that they didn't need to bring anything. She and Dante' had started cooking the night before and were finishing off everything this morning. They had a variety of meats, sides, breads and desserts. The house smelled like a soul food restaurant and everyone was ready to eat. More guests arrived slowly, Big Mike and his wife, Anthony and Chyna, Malik and a few of Dante's other family and friends. Despite Nathan's negative comments and ugly attitude everyone had a good time. Nathan and his family never made it. When the kids tried to call he never bothered to answer the phone.

Chapter 8

"D, do we have to go to Daddy's for Christmas" Semaja asked as she and Dante' sat in the den putting a puzzle together.

"Yeah D, I think we should stay home because it's our first Christmas in our new house and if we go to Miami it will be our first Christmas without Mommy and you won't be there either" Semaj added.

Gerrard looked to Dante' for a response. Dante' looked at him and asked "What are your thoughts?"

"I don't want to go either. I mean, I want to spend time with Dad but I don't want to have to stay at Tia's when he goes to work. I would rather be at home. I was wondering if Mioshi could come here and spend Christmas with us."

"We'll talk to your Mom about it when she gets home and have her talk it over with your Dad and we'll go from there."

Of course Nathan was totally against it. He argued that Myangel had the kids for Thanksgiving so it's only fair that he gets them for Christmas. He also said there is no way in hell that Mioshi was coming to New York for Christmas. The closer and closer it got to Christmas the more the kids voiced their disinterest in going to Nathan's. Myangel hated to be the bearer of bad news telling the kids that Nathan wasn't going for them staying home so she tried to put it off as long as possible. She called a week before Christmas to find out what day he would arrive to pick the kids up.

"He hasn't called you" Tia asked.

"No, what's going on"

"He's in jail, sitting out some tickets."

"Tickets? He too cheap to pay to get out?"

"He didn't want me to tell anyone where he was."

"And what were you supposed to tell the kids when he didn't show up to get them?"

"I asked him that. He told me not to worry about it because the kids didn't want to come here no way. Mioshi really wants to see them."

"We invited you guys over for Thanksgiving and Christmas."

"Really"

"Yes, I mean I know it's not ideal but at least the kids get to spend time with each other. When he put up a big fuss about Thanksgiving I knew he wasn't coming for Christmas so I asked if we could get Mioshi."

"Really? This is the first I'm hearing about all this. Mioshi would love to come to New York with you guys. That's all she ever talks about. I wouldn't feel comfortable, especially without Nathan being there, besides it's not like the family cares too much for me anyway."

"Well, it's not like you're going anywhere. You are Mioshi's mother, might as well get used to it."

"Give me a few days to think it over. I'll call you and let you know."

Myangel wasn't surprised when Tia called her back the next day to tell her she wouldn't make it but that they're more than welcome to get Mioshi until the weekend before school started back. Myangel made arrangements for Tia to come to New York when Margaret and Sal came.

When Mioshi arrived she was attached to Myangel just as she had been when she was a baby. She also latched on to Dante'. He was really good with the kids and had no problem getting her to interact with him. Christmas went off without error. All of the kids were happy with the many gifts they received.

One of Myangel's gifts from Dante' was an engagement ring in which he had the kids assistance picking out.

"Mommy, this is a gift from all of us. Me, Jas, Gerrard, Semaja and D. We love you very, very much" Semaj told her as he smiled big before passing it to her.

The ring had been attached to the ribbon holder for a picture the five of them had taken and blown up. Originally she was going to pull the string and get right to the picture until she saw the sparkles for the ring. She saw the diamonds on the ring and went wild. She rubbed her hand across the ring and looked over at Dante' with a smile, realizing that it was indeed an engagement ring.

"Okay Mommy" Semaja said as she came and stood in front of her "we were wondering if you would like to marry Dante' because he would sho nuff like to marry you. Right, Dante?"

Dante' wasn't weak, seeing the kids happiness about this moment brought tears to his eyes. He knew that marrying Myangel meant that he was also marrying them and he welcomed them all. Without hesitation he said "Yeah Bebe" as he got down on his knees and took the ring and her hand in his, "Will you marry me?"

"Yes" she squealed. "Of course I will. I love you so much."

"Yay" the kids screamed. "She said yes. Mommy said yes. Whoo hoo" Gerrard yelled.

Margaret was wiping at her own tears and just as happy. Sal was happy as well but in the back of his mind he knew Nathan hadn't yet showed his ass. When he gets hold of the news there was no doubt in his mind that things were going to get critical.

"I'm so happy for Myangel. Dante' is so good for her and he loves the kids just like they're his own" Margaret was telling Sal on their ride home a few days later. Mioshi was not ready to leave and cried herself to sleep in the backseat.

"I'm happy for her too, for all of them."

"But what?"

"What do you mean 'but what'?"

You're happy for her but there is something else you want to say. What is it?"

"It's nothing. Do you want to stop off and grab a bite to eat?"

"No, I'm fine."

An hour or so later Margaret brought up the proposal again. "That ring was beautiful, wasn't it?"

"Yeah it was. She deserves it."

"She really does. Even if it didn't come from Nathan. I mean I like Dante', he's great for her like I said but I still had high hopes that she and Nathan would get back together."

"Well"

"I don't know what to say about him. Even after all the chances Myangel gave him he still hasn't straightened up. Not only that but he hasn't bothered to admit that he's the cause of his own problems. He blames everybody but himself. He blames Myangel for starting up with Dante'. He blames the kids and us for liking him, for being in agreement with their relocation, for everything."

"What do you think he's going to have to say about the engagement?"

"Who gives a shit? I mean, I know he will be bothered by it but just like everything else that lead up to this, he will just have to get over it."

"Sounds good and easy as hell but it won't be that easy."

"None of this has been easy. Him cheating wasn't easy, Mioshi wasn't easy. The divorce wasn't easy. None of it was easy for any of us but we've accepted it and we've moved on. He needs to take responsibility for his actions and move on too."

"Yeah that's what he needs to do at this point."

Later that night after Margaret had taken some time to think about what Sal had to say regarding Nathan's possible reaction to Myangel's engagement she called Myangel.

"Hey baby girl, do you have a minute"

"Sure Mom, what's going on? Is everything okay?"

"Yes, congratulations on your engagement. You truly deserve it and Dante' is perfect for you."

"Aww, thanks Mom."

"The kids really love him. We all do."

"Yes and that is such a blessing."

Margaret held the phone for a minute without saying anything.

"Look Mom, I know what your concern is and it's only natural. Nathan won't be nowhere near as happy as everyone else. I know this and I'm sure his feelings will be hurt but I've lived a nice chunk of my life for Nathan. I tried to make him happy. I tried to be understanding. I tried to be forgiving. I tried everything for him, for us. Things didn't work out in spite of all that. It bothered me at first. I blamed myself. Asked myself over and over if there was more I could have done, if there was something I did wrong. The more chances I gave him the more he showed me that things had just run their course. I've accepted that and I've moved on."

"I know baby, and it's not you. You're doing the right thing. I just…"

"I know Mom, I know. I'll tell Nathan. Hopefully Mioshi won't tell Tia before I get a chance to speak with him. I've already discussed it with Dante'. Would like to let Nathan know as soon as possible, go ahead and get it out of the way so that it can marinate for a while. No reason to have secrets between us."

"You won't tell him by phone will you?"

"I thought about it, but no. I'm bringing the kids to see my brother's baby before school starts back. I know Nate is home now so I think it's best we meet face to face and discuss all this."

"And Dante' is okay with this?"

"Yes, he has no problem with me talking to Nathan at all. It's the drama he has a problem with and I can't blame him. That's why we both agreed that it would *be best for Nathan to hear it from me. Dante' will come to Miami with us. He refuses to be in New York when I tell Nathan however, he did agree that he does not have to be with me, seeing as how that would only add fuel to the fire."*

"Okay, so when exactly will you all make it here?"

"January 2nd. We will bring in the new year at home together and then head out for Miami on a plane that morning."

"Okay."

"Mom, don't worry yourself. Everything is going to be okay in due time."

Chapter 9

Nathan was glad Myangel called him up to meet her for lunch. Mioshi had mentioned that she overheard an argument between Myangel and Dante' the other night. He was hoping things would finally be over with between the two of them and that she was coming to him to let him know. Even though she told him she planned to put the house up for sale he'd convinced her not to just yet. He gave her some bogus excuse as to the reason why but in his head he figured that one day they would be one big happy family again.

"Hey, wassup" he asked as he walked up behind her in the line for a seat at Cheddar's.

"Hey" she said as she accepted the hug he offered. "You're late, as usual."

"At least I'm consistent."

"That you are" she laughed.

"Table for two" the waitress asked?

"Yes please."

"What would you two like to drink?"

"I'll have a frozen Margarita swirl with salt around the rim and a glass of water. Nate, what about you?"

"I'll take a Heineken."

"Any appetizers for you today?"

"Spinach dip" they said at the same time.

Nathan looked at her and smiled. She smiled back while thinking in her head that things were off to a good start.

"Where my babies at?"

"They're with Anthony."

"You see your new nephew yet?"

"Yeah, he's so adorable. Looks just like Anthony's peanut head butt."

Soon their drinks and spinach dip were out on the table and their main course had been ordered. Nathan asked more questions like how long they planned to be in town. How did they bring in the new year and if she had any New Year's resolutions. Small talk.

By the time their food was placed in front of them Nathan was ready to get down to the real reason for their meeting. He was anxious to tell her all the plans he had already set in place for them to return to Miami.

Myangel received a text message from Chyna that said "I'm moving to New York, seriously." Myangel's response was "I knew it wouldn't be long. I'm in town. Will call you in a little bit."

"Why you got that look on your face?"

"Chyna says she's moving to New York."

"Oh yeah, that's the move for everybody huh? Just up and run away from things. What's up with New York though" Nathan asked as he stuck his fork into Myangel's plate to sample her broccoli.

"Up and run away" she asked "so you think she's just up and running away without good reason? And why do you say running? Why can't she just be walking?"

Nathan looked at her with a smirk.

"You ran"

"I didn't run Nathan. But that's irrelevant now."

"I know, so wassup? What, you couldn't tell me over the phone? You haven't been too interested in seeing my face in a long time."

"You act as if you've given me reason to want to be anywhere near you."

"What you mean?"

"You and your bipolar attitudes. You have mood swings worse than a female when things don't go your way."

"I'll take that cause I know I been on one lately. I ain't feeling the way shits been going but all that's about to change."

"Oh, you gone switch it up on us? I hope it's for the better."

"Oh yeah, always for the better baby. Always. Things will be just as they should be."

"That's good to know, I guess."

"You're looking fly as ever ma, for real. What a nigga wouldn't give to be all up on you right now" he said as he leaned across the table a little to get closer to her face.

"Nathan, I hate to say I told you so but honey I told you your ass would miss me when I'm gone."

"Yeah you said that. I mean wassup though, when we gone stop playing all these games and get our shit in order?"

"Our shit Nathan? Don't you mean when will you get your shit in order?"

"I did some things to set the shit in motion, true enough. I did that, but you did that too. So I'm saying, what we gone do about it? How can I make this shit right?"

Tia called Nathan's phone asking him where he was. He said "I told you I was going to holla at Marko about some business. Chill out on all that calling and texting me. You buggin" he said before hanging up.

"Why you lie?"

"I guess I'm supposed to just tell her I'm meeting you for lunch?"

"Why not? It's not like there is anything going on between the two of us."

"Not yet anyway."

"Whatever Nathan, look I wanted to be the first to tell you that..."

"That what" he was asking as some chick stopped by the table to tell her baby to say hi to Uncle Nate.

"Hi Uncle Nate"

"Wassup lil man, I haven't seen you since you were a baby."

Myangel looked at the little boy closely and shook her head. Nathan saw her and knew exactly what she was thinking before she even said anything.

"Is this Anthony's son?"

"Who are you" the chick asked with a hint of attitude.

"Oh my God, say it ain't so" This little boy looked to be maybe 2 years younger than the twins.

"It is so, who are you and why do you want to know" the chick asked with her hands now on her hips as she held her son close to her.

Nathan didn't want to be the one to tell Anthony's business so instead of him making introductions he ordered another beer.

"Excuse me, I'm Myangel. I'm Anthony's sister" she said to the woman in front of their table. To the little boy she said *"I'm your auntie. Wow."*

The chick looked from Nathan to Myangel, to the little boy, to Myangel, the little boy and then back to Myangel again. *"I'm Roxi, I apologize. I'm just so use to females giving me beef and..."*

"I know. How old are you" she addressed the little boy. *"What's your name?"*

"De Anthony" he was saying as Anthony and the kids walked into the restaurant.

Turns out the chick and her son were supposed to be meeting Anthony there with his new son and his nieces and nephews. He hadn't planned on Myangel and

Nathan being there. Neither he nor Nathan planned on seeing the chick's twin sister Rosi, who also had a son by Nathan. Their son was around the same age.

"Fuck" Nathan said when he saw her headed in their direction. He put his head down even though he'd already been spotted.

Myangel turned around to look over her shoulder and saw the little boy. The little boy had the same face as Jasara and the twins, the same face as Nathan.

"Fuck" also came out of Anthony's mouth.

Turns out they had been keeping each other's secrets.

Myangel laughed as she stood up tossing her napkin into her unfinished plate of food. "And to think I was worried about keeping secrets from you" she said as she glanced briefly in Nathan's direction before turning to Anthony. "And you, I never would have expected this from you, but then too I never expected...you know what, forget it."

She turned her attention to Rosi "Hi, I'm Myangel. Apparently we share something in common, a lot in common. I'm his baby mama she said as she pointed to Nathan and his sister she said as she looked in Anthony's direction. And these are our children "Jasara, Semaja, Semaj and Gerrard"

"Are you guys staying with your Dad and Uncle or are you going with me?"

"Umm, we will stay with Uncle" Gerrard said as he looked at his mom closely.

"Mommy are you okay?"

"I'm fine baby. Keep an eye on your brother and sisters and don't give your Uncle no trouble." To Anthony she said "Call me when you're ready for me to pick them up." To Nathan she rolled her eyes before announcing "By the way, I'm getting married" she said as she flashed her engagement ring. "Good day" she said with a smile as she walked away.

Chapter 10

Chyna was calling as she walked out the door. *"Where are you?"*

"I'm at home, where are you?"

"Leaving Cheddars"

"I was just on my way up there."

"You don't want that. Decide on something else and let me know where to meet you at."

"What's going on?"

"Nothing. I want to see you."

Let's go to Buffalo Wild Wings."

Good, I could use a few drinks. See you there."

She dialed Dante' after hanging up. *"How did it go" he asked.*

Where are you?"

Me and Malik about to hit up Buffalo Wild Wings to catch the game."

"Oh really, so are Chyna and I."

You're going to watch the game?"

"No, I'm going to have a few drinks. Chyna is going to eat and since you and Malik will be there we can watch you two."

"You still didn't tell me how it went"

"We'll talk when I get there."

Myangel couldn't help but laugh at the turn of events. "God, you have a wonderful sense of humor."

Dante' took one look at Myangel before pulling her into his arms. "I take it everything went well."

"Better than ever" she said as she kissed his lips. After giving Malik a hug she escorted them to their booth. "Chyna hasn't made it yet but she should be walking in the door at any minute."

Nathan and Anthony were both calling Myangel's phone trying to explain. She had gathered from texts that they were still together trying to come up with a master plan. She ignored their calls and text Gerrard instead. 'Call Mommy when you're ready for me to come pick you up or if you need me." His reply was 'Okay Mommy ☺

"What's up" Dante' was asking as Chyna walked into the bar area looking around.

She finger waved at her and stood to hug her when she walked up. Everyone placed their drink and food orders. Just as the waitress walked off Dante' again asked "What's up?"

She looked to Chyna and said "Sis, I don't know how to say this."

"Say what?"

She grabbed a hold to Dante's hand up under the table to assure him that she wasn't ignoring him. "I met up with Nathan today at Cheddar's to tell him that Dante' and I are engaged. Before we got around to discussing this a chick walks up and tells her son to "Tell Uncle Nate hi" It took a minute for me to look at the little boy and for it to register in my head that he looks just like Anthony and is maybe 2 years younger than the twins." She reached out to Chyna with her other hand.

"Wow" was all Chyna could say.

"My sentiments exactly but that's not it."

"What else could there possibly be?"

"Anthony comes strolling in with his new baby" she laughs "and the kids. I'm facing their direction and Nathan is facing the other direction. He doesn't see what I see and I don't see what he sees but all of a sudden he says "Fuck" I turn around to see what his 'Fuck' is in reference to and this other chic is walking up. She's an identical twin to the first chick and she also has a little boy. This one looks just like Semaja, Semaj and Jasara" she laughs. "Now Anthony says 'Fuck'."

"Are you fucking serious" Chyna asks

"Dead ass"

Myangel knew that Chyna, even though she had already made the decision to leave Anthony and move to New York, was still upset. She knew that Chyna had just learned of the most recent baby. What probably hurt most was the fact that Anthony kept telling her it was her fault that they hadn't had babies and because he now had two that she was aware of she started believing it. Myangel and Dante' talked about everything so he assumed the same thing and wanted to give the women time to talk.

To Malik he said "Let's go shoot some pool man."

"Chyna I'm so sorry. I know this is just…"

"It's just too much"

Myangel moved to be closer to Chyna in the booth and wrapped her arms around her. "I won't lie and say it's going to be easy but I can promise you that it does get better with time. I'm a witness" she said as she wiped away at Chyna's tears.

"What about you" she asked as she looked at Myangel "doesn't this shit just open up old wounds for you"

"No honey, really, it just serves as confirmation that I did the right thing by moving on. I'm happy with Dante'. I love that man and he doesn't measure my love by how much of his shit I can deal with. I don't have to tell him what his responsibilities are, what my needs are over and over. He listens to me, he pays attention and he just wants me to be happy. I want the same and do the same for

him. That's all I ever wanted, someone to love me unconditionally and Dante' does that. Not only does he love me, but he loves my kids too. Who could ask for anything more?"

Chyna smiled in spite of her tears. She was happy for Myangel. Not only happy but seeing the outcome of Myangel's situation gave her hope that there was real love out there.

"Does Anthony know you're moving to New York?"

" I told him but of course he doesn't believe me."

"Of course not, actions speak louder than words. Don't get me wrong, I had high hopes that things would work out between you and Anthony, really I did. Just as I thought things would work out between Nathan and me but after a length of time I just had to see things for what it was. Just as you do, it hurts but sis, it is what it is. Had it not been for you and Anthony being together the two of us probably never would have met. Had we not been going through what we were going through we never could have bonded the way that we have. So, as bad as things look we still have to see the blessings in all this."

"Yeah you're right" Chyna said as Malik walked up on her and kissed her lips. "You coming home with me tonight."

"Yeah"

"I wasn't asking you ma, I was telling you."

Myangel smiled as she looked at Dante' adoringly. "I love you man" she said before tonguing him down.

Big Mike called Myangel up and asked "Oh is this how we doing it now. You and the fam come in to town and don't holla at me? Where they do that at?"

"I'm sorry big bro. I was on a mission. But I'm on my way to see you now. The kids are with Dante'. It's just me and Chyna right now."

They were sitting on the front porch drinking on a few beers when Anthony, Nathan and Bishop pulled up.

"Aww damn" Myangel said when she looked up. She had been avoiding Nathan. She had made peace with Anthony after cussing him out real good.

Chyna looked up and rolled her eyes.

Nathan walked up and said "Say Mya, let me holla at you for a minute."

"Nathan, not now" she said as she fired up a blunt.

"Where the kids at" Anthony asked?

"Dante' took them bowling."

"Why you ain't with them" Nathan asked

"You see what I'm doing" she left it at that before Big Mike said "Damn sis, that's a big ass rock you got on your finger. You holding out on me."

He smiled big "I see ya doing big thangs."

Unlike everyone else Big Mike didn't try to sugarcoat things for Nathan's sake. Nathan continuously fucked up and didn't consider his consequences, now he's facing them. "When did D pop the question?"

"Christmas"

"You never finished telling me how he did it" Chyna said as she looked at her.

She explained how he and the kids had everything planned out. How they picked out the ring together and proposed together. She wore a huge smile on her face as she gave a detailed description. Nathan watched her closely. Of all the outcomes he could have hoped for on the day they met for lunch he sure didn't expect it to turn out the way it did. Had Rosi not shown up with Nathaniel he was sure there would have been a different outcome.

Big Mike sensed the tension amongst everyone and asked "Fuck wrong with y'all niggas"

Nobody answered at first. Myangel said "I don't know about the rest of y'all but I'm feeling lovely"

I'd feel lovely too if I had that big ass rock on my finger and my fiancé' just won two major cases" Chyna said as she bumped shoulders with Myangel.

Anthony asked "When y'all go home, how long before y'all come back?"

"Probably not until April, the kids will be out for Spring Break then."

"When's the wedding" Bishop asked.

"August 15th"

"August, next year right" Anthony asked.

"No Squeak, as in 9 months from now" Myangel told him.

"You ain't pregnant again, are you?"

"And what if I was?"

"Say Myangel, for real let me holla at you for a minute. No bullshit."

"Nathan, no bullshit. You don't got it like that no mo" she laughed. "What do you have to say? There is nothing that Anthony and Bishop don't know about and everything that goes on Chyna and I talk about. So really, say whatever you need to say and get it over with."

He was about to say something when her cell phone started to ring and she held her finger up for him to hold on a minute. "Yeah baby, what's up?" She listened for a minute. "Yeah I'm still here. Okay, nah that's cool. You sure?" She smiled as she listened to Dante's sexy voice as he gave details regarding his outing with the kids. The kids had so much fun that they all were taking baths and heading to bed. Although Myangel wanted to be with them both she and Dante' felt like it was just as important for Dante' to bond with them alone. Myangel looked to Chyna during the call.

"Alright heffa, I already know what you're going to say" she laughed.

"And what is that"

"I ain't saying it out loud."

Myangel laughed again before telling Dante' "Baby I'll be there in like 20 minutes. Do you need me to stop off and pick up anything?" Dante's response was "Hell nah, you know I don't even like you being out this time of night on the cool. We got everything we need here and what we don't have, we don't need. Hurry yo ass up and get here. I got a bone to pick with you." Myangel bit her bottom lip with a smile and glossy eyes. "Yes sir, see you shortly. I love you too babe."

She stood up and said "Alright peeps, y'all know me love you long time but I need to go see my man about a mule and..."

"Get yo ass on out of here" Big Mike told her as he playfully popped the back of her neck. "Y'all be safe. Love you sis."

"Love you too bro" she said as she hugged him. She kissed Anthony's cheek and told him "I love you too big head secret keeping chump."

"Love you sis, you better fucking answer the phone when I call or text you too."

"Or else what she asked"

"There's gone be some consequences and repercussions"

"A little late for that, don't you think"

Bishop was next up in line so she said "Alright B, it was good seeing you. Stay out of trouble."

"You see who I'm with, I ain't getting in no trouble."

Laughing Myangel said "Messing with these two you'll have babies all over the place." She stood directly in front of Nathan and smacked the shit out of him. Caught him and everybody else completely off guard. "I've been wanting to do that and so much more for a long, long time." She leaned forward and kissed his cheek with a wicked smile "Love you too Nate." She walked to the car without another word.

"Will somebody tell me what the fuck going on" Big Mike asked

"I want to know too" Bishop said as he looked to Anthony and Nathan for a response.

"Man, Rosi and Roxi showed up at Cheddars the other day." Nathan said

"The twins y'all used to mess with" Big Mike asked.

"Yeah, the one that nigga got a baby by" Bishop said as he pointed in Anthony's direction. "And the one this nigga" he said as he pointed in Nate's direction "paid to have an abortion."

"An abortion that she never had" Nathan said as he took the blunt that was being passed around.

"So how Mya find out?"

"Me and her was having lunch and Roxi came through, was telling De Anthony to tell Uncle Nate hi and the next thing I know Mya done figured that out and then Rosi come in behind her. Before she could even see Nathaniel I'm like fuck."

"What y'all was meeting up for"

"So she could show me her ring and tell me she getting married, said she didn't want me to have to hear it from somebody else."

"And you know her and Chyna thick as thieves so she told Chyna and she come calling me up talking about she moving to New York and shit" Anthony added.

"Y'all niggas stay fucking up" Big Mike told them.

"Me and Chyna agreed we should see other people."

"Because you were already seeing other people nigga. Fuck you expect. Told you to stay single" Bishop told Anthony. "And you nigga, you done fucked around and messed up the best thing you ever had going. No bullshit" he said to Nathan.

Like back when Marko tried to talk some sense into him, Nathan let it go in one ear and out the other.

Chapter 11

The next day Nathan text Myangel, 'I don't appreciate you putting your hands on me.' Dante' was the one to read the message. Myangel's main focus when she got to the room was sexing Dante' like crazy so they never got around to discussing what went on at Big Mike's.

"Bebe" he called out from his spot on the sofa.

"Yeah baby" she asked from the kitchen where she was making steak fajitas.

"Let me holla at you for a minute"

"Yes sir" she asked as she leaned over the back of the couch and kissed his lips.

The kids were on the floor and together they were watching 'The Perfect Holiday'. Dante' pulled the text message up and showed it to her then turned around to see her reaction. She laughed before saying "Yeah I did it."

Dante' looked at her and laughed too. He watched her walk back into the kitchen. After all this time he still loved everything about her. Every minute of every day he fell in love with her over and over again. Nathan kept texting her and he kept watching her from the kitchen. He wasn't stressing over the text messages from Nathan and Myangel heard her phone going off and didn't seem the least bit concerned. He got up from the sofa and made his way into the kitchen entryway. He stood there watching her before he started to sing Musiq's So Beautiful as he walked up on her and kissed her neck. He continued to sing as he chopped up onions and bell peppers to brown in a skillet.

"Thanks sexy baby" Myangel said as she kissed his cheek.

After the kids were off to bed Myangel and Dante' relaxed in the living room sipping on Tequila.

"Have you decided where you want to get married at yet woman?"

"The Lighthouse at Chelsea Piers"

"In New York"

"What do you mean, in New York? What's wrong with that?"

"Nothing's wrong with it baby. I just thought you might want to get married in Miami."

"Why, I mean everybody I want to come won't mind traveling to New York."

"The Lighthouse is a nice place babe. Good choice. I'm diggin it."

"You diggin it" she asked as she relaxed on top of him.

"Yeah Bebe, so you got some ideas in mind of the color and setup for the venue? All that good stuff."

"I was thinking we could figure it all out together."

"What do you think about cream and plum?"

"Ooh I love it baby" she said as she visualized her wedding dress in her head and Dante' in his tuxedo, the kids all dressed and ready for the big day.

"Have you mentioned the date to anyone?"

"Of course I've discussed it with Mom and Chyna. I told Anthony, Big Mike and Nathan the other day."

"The day you slapped him?"

"Yes"

"Why you slap him?"

"He lucky I didn't shoot his ass."

"What did he do when you slapped him? Who was around?"

"It was me, my brothers, him and his friend and Chyna. I slapped him and he didn't do nothing. He wasn't expecting it, nobody was."

The rest of Winter break went off without error. Nathan called every day to speak with the kids and didn't seem at all confrontational to Myangel. She knew it had a lot to do with finding out about Nathaniel. By the time the kids were back in school the text messages had stopped. Everyone was relaxing and adjusting to work and school life again. Myangel and the kids had been in and out of town since before their move to New York. She and Dante' agreed to cut back on traveling, unless of course Nathan wanted the kids in Miami. In that case things would be worked out between the two of them. The kids were in to sports, choir, band and as a family they volunteered with a local family shelter.

Chapter 12

Myangel dialed Dante's number just as he walked through the door at home.

"Hey sexy daddy, I was just about to call you."

"Oh yeah" he asked as he kissed her lips as she chopped fresh vegetables to make a chicken stir fry.

"Yep, your mom called. She's coming to spend a few weeks with us. Tonight she's taking the kids to visit Diane."

"Everything okay?"

"Yeah, why wouldn't it be?"

"Just making sure. So what we got planned?"

"Chyna called, her and Malik are going to the Aqua Bar. I figured we could join them. We haven't been out in a while. You cool with that?"

"Sounds like a plan. What time we leaving" he asked as he started a trail of kisses from the back of her ear to her neck.

"Well after we shower and eat, or eat and shower"

"Good, so we have plenty of time to get it in" he said as he turned the fire off under the skillet, took the knife from her hand and lead her into their bedroom.

"Mom and the kids already left right?"

"Yes"

Myangel ran into a chick Anthony used to go to high school with while at Aqua that night. At the time she and Chyna were out on the dance floor as usual.

"Myangel, girl is that you? Oh my God, look at you. You look fabulous" she said as she gave cheek kisses.

"Yvette, hey what's up? How you been?"

"I'm good. How are you? I haven't seen you in years. I thought I heard you had kids."

"I do, 4 now."

"You don't look like you have no kids at all. Damn Ma, what you do to make it all snap back like that?"

"I work out and try to eat healthy. The kids keep me active and I don't know, guess it never really got a chance to sit on me."

The two stood around talking a little while longer before Myangel and Chyna made their way back up to VIP where Dante' and Malik were. They started passing a blunt between the 4 of them and enjoying their time together while sippin drinks.

It wasn't long before Yvette got in touch with Anthony. She mentioned seeing Myangel in the club with her friend, gave a detailed description of who she was with and what they were doing. Anthony didn't think much of it the first time. He just assumed Chyna was hanging out with Myangel and Dante' brought one of his boys along. After the initial conversation Yvette and Anthony kept in touch. They often talked about him coming through New York and the two of them hooking up. Eventually she made her way to Miami and the two of them hit it off real good. She and her homegirls would get together to make regular trips to Miami to kick it with Anthony. Yvette tried her best to get in good with Myangel but they just weren't in to the same things. Although a few times they ran into each other in this club or the mall, they still never became the "good friends" that Chyna and Myangel had become.

It wasn't long before Anthony was making his way to New York. Nathan decided he'd pop in on Myangel and the kids to see how things were going in their world. Yvette and some of her friends were hanging out at the strip club when Anthony and Nathan came through. It was a well-known hang out spot and everybody that was anybody was up there that night, including Dante' and Malik.

Nathan and Anthony were pretty fucked up by the time Myangel and Chyna rolled up in the spot. By the time Anthony saw Chyna she was all hugged up with Malik. Nathan spotted Myangel at the same time. She was sitting in Dante's lap and the two were locked in some mean lip service. Anthony excused himself from the table he sat at and made his way in the direction Myangel and her crew was in.

"What up sis"

"Anthony" she said as she turned around to look at him. She stood up and gave him a hug. They talked about how long he would be in town and why he didn't call to let her know he was coming. He looked in Chyna's direction and said "What up Chyna, I see you" as he leaned over to kiss her cheek. He dapped up Dante' and sat around chopping it up a minute. He was a little bothered seeing Chyna all hugged up with another nigga but he reminded himself that they did agree to see other people. Before walking away from the table he and Myangel made plans to get together before he left town.

When he walked back over to his own table Nathan asked "What they got going on over there?"

"Aww ain't nothing, they just chillin on it" he said as he sat down and took the drink Yvette had just ordered for him.

Nathan sat back a little while longer still watching Myangel although he tried to appear unaffected. It wasn't long before he was up out his seat headed in their direction. Dante' had spotted Nathan before Anthony walked up so he wasn't surprised when he showed his face.

"Yo what up fam" he asked as he looked from Myangel and Dante' to Chyna and Malik.

"Hey Nate" Myangel said without moving from her spot in Dante's lap. Chyna said what's up before standing up to give him a brief hug.

Nathan extended his hand to Dante' and Myangel watched Nathan closely to see where his head was at. The two shook hands. Anthony had no idea what was going on but didn't want to be too far away if Nathan decided to get out of pocket. He made his way over, Yvette and her friends followed behind him.

When Yvette noticed Myangel she introduced her friends to her and in the midst of all this Dante' told Nathan, "Let me holla at you for a minute."

They both excused themselves and took a walk. Dante' felt that he and Nathan had danced around each other long enough. He didn't feel the need to try and let Nathan know he wasn't going anywhere. By now his actions should have proven that. Regardless of how everything went down and for what reason the bottom line was still that the two of them needed to establish some form of communication for the kids' sake. Dante' reasoned that if the shoe were on the other foot he would make amends with the dude for the simple fact that his kids were around him every day. Although Nathan tried to act like it didn't bother him any more Dante' felt like he did his part and he would just see how things would turn out.

Chapter 13

Valentine's Day fell on a weekend. A weekend in which Nathan asked to have the kids. He called that Friday to say he had arrived in New York and would get the kids after they got home from school. Dante' and Myangel had plans to spend the weekend in a cabin along with Chyna, Malik and a few other friends. The plan was for Myangel to be ready around 4 and they would leave out as soon as the kids left.

Nathan showed up without calling. Gerrard called out from her bedroom "Mommy, Daddy's at the door."

"What, are you sure? He didn't call first."

"Mom, he never calls ahead whenever he knows D's not at home."

"Okay baby, get the door for me. I'll be out in a minute."

Before Myangel could get into her body moisturizing ritual good Nathan started to complain about how he had plans and needed to get going.

Myangel grabbed her terry cloth robe and secured the strings tightly before making her way out of her bedroom and into the hallway. She grabbed the bags she had packed for the kids weekend trip with their dad.

"Well damn Mya, it took you long enough" Nathan was saying before he even bothered looking up from his phone.

"I know Gerrard told you I was in the shower. You always gotta be difficult. You could have waited a few minutes."

"A few minutes for what" he asked as he looked up. "What else you have to do?"

"I packed everything in one bag. All except for Jasara's bottles and food." Myangel passed the bag over to him.

"What time I have to bring them back on Monday?"

"Any time is cool. Just call to make sure we're home. What you have planned for them?"

"Why, you trying to roll with us? Go get dress. Come kick it with the fam."

"We already made plans but you guys have fun" she said as she kissed the kids and reminded them to behave. Everybody was standing to leave and giving hugs. Nathan reached out to hug Myangel just as Dante' walked into the den area. Myangel was pulling away from Nathan but he wrapped his arms around her and hugged her close.

Dante' looked on with a mug on his face but didn't address the issue when the kids came rushing over to him. Although he was interacting with the kids he noticed that Myangel was in her robe and noticed the way Nathan was looking at her. He wasn't at all comfortable with the situation.

"Hey baby" she said as she walked over to him and kissed his lips. "I'm glad you're here. Can you see them out while I finish getting dressed, please"

She didn't wait for a response before leaving the room. It wasn't long before Nathan and the kids were out the door and Dante' was heading back to their bedroom. He walked into the bathroom to find Myangel completely naked while smoothing her body over with cocoa butter baby oil gel. He stood watching her while licking his lips. Seeing the robe on the counter beside her he looked into her eyes.

"You ain't have nothing on up under that robe while you was out there entertaining?"

"Entertaining? Come on D, be for real. He came without calling and I happened to be in the shower. I told G to get the door and I would be out in a minute. My intention was to do what I'm doing now and throw something on before going out there but he was being impatient saying he had plans. I tried to get

everything in order for him so they could be on their way and I could be ready when you got here."

Dante' didn't respond. Myangel looked at him closely and asked "Why you got that frown on your face?"

"No reason Bebe, I'm good. You good?"

"Yeah I'm good."

"Well hurry yo sexy ass up then before we get caught up in traffic."

Anthony was in New York on one of his many visits to see Yvette. He invited Myangel out to lunch just the two of them. It was the first outing the two shared alone in a long time.

"So what's up with you and Yvette" she asked him before sipping on her Margarita swirl.

"Ain't nothing but the usual. We just kick it from time to time."

"She's been calling me a lot lately trying to hook up. I told her I would get with her next week for bowling with some of her homegirls."

"You know she trying her best to get on your good side. I told her what was up with me and Chyna way back when and she see that the two of you are close and don't want no issues."

"What does me and Chyna being friends have to do with me and her?"

"She trying to be next in line, so she say" Anthony said with a smirk.

Myangel looked at him a minute and told him "You really should give it a rest. After this last go round you don't think you need to be single until you're really serious about settling down?"

"Why you say it like that?"

"Because y'all niggas think it's cool to be smiling all in a chick's face claiming to love her and telling her you want to spend the rest of your life with her.

Meanwhile you fucking Mesha, Kesha and Tesha over cross town telling them the same shit."

"It ain't even that serious with me and Yvette."

"It's never serious for you but that don't stop you from allowing them to think that it is."

"They think what they want to think, that's on them."

Myangel sat there shaking her head. "You just don't get it."

"What is there to get sis?"

"When your daughter grows up and gets her heart broken by some nigga just like you and Nathan then you will finally understand what I mean."

"You said that like you still fucked up about it. Let me find out" he laughed.

"Whatever."

"Good thing I ain't got no daughters to worry about."

"No shit."

"I don't know why you frontin like you wasn't out there doing dirt too. You all the time talking about us niggas breaking hearts. What about what you did and still doing?"

"You and I both know I didn't start up with Dante' until after I was pregnant with the twins."

"I don't know that for sure. I just know what you been telling us all these years. Bro say y'all was kicking it way before then."

"Of course he saying that now. He'll say anything to justify his actions, or at least attempt to."

"So if what we doing is so wrong then why was you fucking off on him? Y'all was married. You just as wrong as I am."

"You really gone sit here with that lame ass excuse? I guess that's supposed to shut me up? You must have forgotten who I am."

"Nah, never that but I'm saying though you act like you all innocent and shit. How does one situation justify the other?"

" What went down between me and Nathan was a reaction to his actions. It took a long time for it to play out the way that it did and when it did go down it wasn't on no sneak shit. I warned Nathan time and time again. He didn't take heed. That was his bad."

"So you just came right out and told the nigga you was gone fuck around with Dante'?"

"I told him his shit was over the top and to calm the fuck down. I also said that if he didn't we would have an open relationship. I told him I wasn't fucking Dante' yet but that I would be fucking Dante' if he kept fucking around. We both know how it all went down. No need to sugarcoat it now because it is what it is."

"You worse than a fucking nigga for real. I know you got Chyna on that bullshit too."

"Chyna is a grown ass woman. A smart one at that. Game recognize game" she laughed.

Chapter 14

Once back in Miami Anthony was out kicking it with Nathan at the car wash when Chyna called Anthony. She was calling to let him know his mail was being forwarded to her address and that she was sending it by Myangel.

Nathan knew it was Chyna on the phone. So after Anthony finished his call he asked "Y'all still cool?"

"Hell yeah, we ended on good terms. I mean you know she still a little salty about the babies but we agreed to see other people before that all came out."

"And her fucking this nigga in New York ain't got you feeling some type of way?"

"Nah, I'm good. We chillin. And who said they fuckin"

"Come on nigga, it's me you talking to. Save your game face for somebody else. I'm already knowing how it is" Nathan told him as he laughed.

Anthony laughed too, "Yeah bro that shit caught a nigga off guard, no doubt. I would have never expected no shit like this from Chyna. I thought she was gone stay down forever, no matter what."

"Man" Nathan said as he eyed a chick that pulled up in a Cadillac CTS similar to the one Myangel used to drive back in the days. In an instant he took a trip down memory lane remembering how things were before it all fell down.

"Yo bro, what's up? You spaced out for a minute there" Anthony told him when he got his attention. "You good?"

"Yeah I'm straight"

"I asked my sister how long her and Dante' was messing around before she got pregnant. She said they didn't start kicking it until around the time she got pregnant with the twins. Said she told you what was what."

"She said that shit and she did that shit. But man I wasn't trying to hear that shit. I was out doing my own thang and she stuck it out after all that time so I just figured she would stick to the script. I never figured she would be confused about who Jasara belonged to and I sure as hell never expected us to be apart, for her to be with this other nigga. I never expected her to move her ass to New York, to take my kids with her to live with this nigga. Now she talking about marriage. Shits fucked up."

Later that night Nathan was really in his feelings. He called Gerrard's cell phone to talk with the kids. He was trying to get a feel for what was going on in their house, whether or not Dante' was home. It wasn't long before he got his answer. Semaja asked *"Mommy when is D coming home?"*

"He should be here in another hour or so. Why baby? What's wrong?"

"I want to stay up until he gets home. I have something to tell him."

"Really, and what's that?"

" It's a secret."

"A secret you're keeping from me" she asked with a smile.

"I have to Mommy. We will tell you later. Okay?" she asked before kissing Myangel's cheek.

Nathan's plan was to send Myangel a few text messages telling her how he was really feeling but between conversations with the kids and Tia in his ear it was hard to get an opening. So that night he had to suck it up. His time to vent would come sooner rather than later.

Dante' had taken the older kids out for pizza while Jasara and Myangel stayed home. He and Gerrard were sitting down having a man to man talk as they have become accustomed to.

"D why don't you and my Daddy get along?"

"We still working through some issues."

"You mean he is. He is working through some issues. I see how you try to be cordial. Is that the right word?"

"Yeah" Dante' said with a smile. "I guess this is just going to take some getting used to for him."

"At the rate he going we all will be grown by then."

Dante' laughed, unsure of what to say at the moment. He didn't have to say anything. Gerrard had more to say.

"And he's always picking fights with Mommy. He blames Mommy for everything that went wrong. Even when Mommy was still being nice to him he was still all mean. Now they don't even really talk to each other."

Dante' listened as Gerrard gave his description of how everything went down. He remembered things as far back as the day they met Nathan. There was love in his voice and Dante' understood that. There was also a lot of pain.

"And that bothers you?"

"Yeah"

"You want them to get back together?"

"No" Gerrard said without having to think it over. " I want you and Mommy to stay together. You make Mommy happy and we're all happy. I just remember how Mommy and Daddy used to get along. It was better then. They don't have to be together to be civil towards each other. And I just think it would be better for everybody if they at least try to get along. Mommy even gets along with Gerald and she used to hate his guts."

Dante' looked at Gerrard acknowledging the young man he was turning into and thankful to be around to witness that growth. "Yeah, you're right. I think it would be better for everybody."

"So you don't have a problem with Mommy talking to Daddy?"

"No, I don't have a problem with them communicating. I just have a problem with the way he talks to her sometimes. I don't like the way he tries to exclude me."

"You do know Mommy doesn't pay him any attention when he does that, right? You also know that she can hold her own and will give Daddy the business if she has to, right?"

"Yeah I know that" Dante' said with a smile.

Semaj and Semaja came back to the table and the conversation ended for the moment.

The conversation started back up later that night as Myangel and Dante' lay in bed watching Steele Magnolias.

"I had a talk with Gerrard today or should I say he had a talk with me."

Myangel laughed "What was this talk about?"

"About communicating, you and Nathan need to communicate more in a civil manner." Before Myangel could interrupt he added "Nathan and I need to learn to communicate period. I mean shit is what it is. Gerrard is right. I ain't going nowhere. Might as well get used to the situation."

"But…"

"No buts Bebe, time to nip this shit in the bud. For Gerrard to come to me with it mean shits serious and I understand where he coming from. This is bigger than us and what we got going on. We gotta do what we gotta do for the kids."

"Kids or not, Nathan is bipolar. One minute he cool and the next he flipping."

"I'd be fucked up in the head too if I wasn't all up in this every night" he said as he smacked her ass "and waking up to you in the morning" Dante said as he kissed Myangel's lips.

"Shut up with your mannish ass"

"I'm saying though, he know he fucked up now. Yeah it took him a minute to fully grasp it but he gets it and he see you moving on, not looking back. He ain't really feeling that shit and it's hitting him hard."

"Well hell, it ain't like I didn't warn him a million times. But enough about him and his issues" she said as she climbed on top of him and rode off into the sunset.

Before leaving for Miami Dante' brought the communication topic up again. "Okay, okay D. I get it and I'll do my part but if he gets out of pocket I'm going off on his ass" Myangel told him calmly.

Chapter 15

Big Mike was supposed to pick them up from the airport but his daughter was having premature labor pains so he was at the hospital. Instead he asked Anthony and Nathan to pick them up. At the time the two of them were in the car together and agreed to be at the airport on time. Big Mike hadn't been able to get a hold to Myangel to tell her the change in plans.

Just as Myangel powered on her cell phone it started to ring. Anthony was calling to find out where they were so he and Nathan could come in for their luggage. She assumed that Anthony had come along with Big Mike and was surprised to see Nathan with him when they did meet up. She had been hoping she would avoid running in to him so soon.

Anthony explained what was going on. Myangel tried calling Big Mike to make sure his daughter was okay. When he didn't answer she sent him a text to call her, to let him know they arrived safely.

It wasn't long before Margaret was calling to get the kids. Anthony wanted to hang out like old times. Myangel mentioned it to Dante' when she called to let him know they arrived safely. His response was "Perfect time to go in a new direction."

One of Anthony's friends was having a barbecue and invited everyone over. Everyone was hanging out, smoking, drinking, playing cards and dominoes. After a while Myangel ducked off to call Dante'. Even though she had just left home she was already missing him. The feeling was mutual. Although he encouraged her to go for the weekend to get the kids settled in and to spend time with her Miami family he was now regretting it as he sat at home alone. The two talked for a good hour before Nathan came looking for her.

"What you doing out here" he asked when he came up behind her as she was ending her phone call. "You alright?"

"I'm good. You alright?"

"Yeah I'm straight" he said as he answered his ringing cell phone. Tia was on the other end. He told her where he was and that he would be home in a few hours.

"Why you got that silly look on your face" he asked Myangel after hanging up.

"I see you do have some truth in you" she laughed.

He laughed too "I see you still got jokes."

Myangel turned to walk into the backyard.

"Oh you just gone walk off like that" he asked in a gentle tone.

She turned around to look at him and asked "What's up?"

"I want to chill with you."

"Nathan you know..."

"I know you in a relationship and I ain't trying to interfere with that" he said as he threw his hands up "but I'm saying though, I ain't just some nigga from cross tracks trying to holla at you."

A group of people walked up and started talking to him. He kept his eyes on Myangel the whole time. She excused herself shortly after.

Anthony and Chyna ended up running off to some club with a few other people at the barbecue. Nathan planned to take Myangel home. Margaret called to let Myangel know that they had arrived back at the house and were cooking breakfast. Myangel hadn't ate at the barbecue and was seriously feeling an omelet, grits and blueberry waffles.

"What's up" Nathan asked

"Mom said they're back at the house and they're cooking breakfast."

"Breakfast, right now?"

"Yes"

"Damn I want some of your waffles. Been craving them like a muthafucka."

"Well the kids just asked me to make some. If you want to stay for dinner you're cool."

"That's what's up."

He called Tia to let her know he was going to hang out with the kids at his old house. Myangel looked over at him and smirked.

"Yeah I learned a little something from my mistakes."

"That's nice to know" she laughed. She knew Tia had no idea she was in town at the moment. None of it really mattered because she had no interest in Nathan aside from the kids but for whatever reason Tia still felt like she was a threat.

When she did find out Myangel was in town the shit would no doubt hit the fan.

"Why don't you invite her and Mioshi over?"
"For what?"

"I mean, we are having a family moment. Don't you think it's time you start trying to incorporate her into this whole set up? I mean, even I'm accepting of it now and I think it's only fair."

Nathan sat and thought it over for a minute. He knew she had a point and Tia had mentioned the same thing on more than one occasion. He decided to just go by the house and scoop them up. He called her and told her "Get ready, about to come through for you and Mioshi." Her response was okay.

"Don't you think you should at least give her a heads up on where you're taking her and that I am here?"

"Why, she got one of two choices Get in and shut up or stay the fuck at home."

"Wow, just like that huh?"

"Hell yeah. You know how I do."

"And I see you still have a lot to learn."

"What?"

"Nothing Nathan."

When he pulled up in front of the condo he shared with Tia he told Myangel to wait in the car while he went inside to get them. Myangel wasn't surprised that Tia decided not to go but encouraged him to take Mioshi with him. He got offended and started talking crazy to her.

Myangel knew Nathan could be a real asshole. She was trying to be the bigger person in the overall situation so she got out the car and asked to speak with Tia alone. She and Tia couldn't be classified as friends but they have been on speaking terms lately concerning the kids.

Tia gave Myangel the same speech she'd given for Christmas, that she knew the family didn't like her and that she didn't feel comfortable or want to cause any problems.

Myangel told her "Honey everyone has accepted you as a part of the family. It's time you make your presence known."

Tia looked at her and said "You seriously don't have a problem with this?"

"No, I don't. Not at all."

Nathan yelled out "If you coming bring your ass on here."

"Nathan" Myangel said in an annoyed tone. To Tia she said "Come on girl, don't pay him no mind."

The kids were happy to see their mother and father together and even happier to see Mioshi. Myangel noticed her kids trying to include Tia in activities that they normally wouldn't have.

Chapter 16

Before leaving New York she and Dante' had a sit down with the kids to discuss the blending of families and how it might be uncomfortable for some people and easier for others. They tried to explain that it would take time, patience and understanding for everything to come together and that it would never be perfect but it had to be done.

Breakfast was good and everyone stayed up pretty late enjoying old cartoons.

Nathan decided that they were staying the night. Everyone was having a good time so Myangel didn't have a problem with it. She only wished Dante' could have come along for this moment. Dante' told her "my time is coming"

She sat outside on the back porch swing alone for a minute until Nathan came out with a blunt.

"Wanna smoke something?"

"Yeah that's cool" she said as she moved her legs from across the swing and sat up straight.

"You alright" he asked

"Do you realize you've asked me that at least 20 times tonight?"

"I'm saying though, you know I'm only asking because I know you."

"What's that supposed to mean?"

"I know you have something to say cause it's written all over your face. So what is it?"

"Nothing, I'm good."

"Quit bullshitten man, what's on your mind?"

"I miss my baby."

"Your babies in there, all of them" he said as he fired up the blunt.

She didn't say anything to him before he passed the blunt. She held on to the blunt long enough for him to look at her and ask again "You sure you alright?"

"I told you I'm good."

"If you was good you wouldn't have that ugly ass look on your face. What's up" he asked as he turned to her with a serious look on his face.

"I miss Dante'. There, I said it."

Nathan held the blunt in his mouth inhaling deeply, saying nothing. When his cell started ringing he automatically assumed Tia was calling from inside the house bitchin. He answered with a hint of attitude. Instead it was Anthony trying to find out where he was and what he was about to get into. Nathan was surprised that Anthony and Chyna were still together when he said they were about to come through. Anthony was just as surprised to hear that Nathan and Myangel were sitting on the back porch together. Nathan didn't go into details about his mom and Tia being there as well.

"Ant about to come through with Chyna."

Myangel's cell phone rang, Dante' was calling to tell her how much he loved her and how he was missing her. He didn't give Myangel time to speak but everything he said put a big kool aid smile on her face. Nathan sat beside her watching her closely.

She ended the call with an "I love you Dante'. Good night" before blowing him a kiss.

"What the fuck that nigga say to have you smiling like that?"

"He told me how much he loves me and what having me in his life means to him."

Nathan got up and walked into the house. Myangel laughed without saying anything to him. He came back out a few minutes later with his weed stash, a bottle of Hennessy and two shot glasses. He passed Myangel the bottle and shot glasses while he rolled a few more blunts. She poured them both a shot.

"Tia didn't want to come out here?"

"She too bougie for the night crawlers"

Myangel laughed "You fool"

After 2 shots and half of another blunt Nathan looked at Myangel and asked "You serious about this nigga huh?"

"You mean Dante'. Say his name, stop referring to him as that nigga" she said with attitude.

"Why I gotta say his name? I'm sure you do enough of that for both of us."

"I sure as hell do, in and out of the bedroom. You're such a character Nate."

"You ain't gone answer my question?"

"You already know the answer to that."

"And you really about to get married?"

"Yes. You and Tia coming to the wedding?"

"What the fuck for? You want me to give you away?"

"That's not a bad idea."

"We smoking the same shit but you must have sniffed something else cause you on cloud 9 for real. What the fuck I look like walking you down the aisle to marry the next nigga?"

"I think it would symbolize a lot"

"A lot of bullshit."

"Nathan, come on now. Why do you have to be so difficult?"

"I'm being difficult because I ain't trying to walk you down the aisle? What the fuck I look like?"

Myangel just looked at him.

"Don't look at me like that. I know you didn't think I was just gone roll with this shit. I ain't feeling it."

"I don't see why not. You should be thrilled."

"Give me one good reason why I should."

"Because you're living the life you chose and I'm accepting of that. You should be accepting of the life I'm choosing. We're both getting what we want and we're both happy."

"Who said I'm happy and what makes you think I'm getting what I want?

"Nate, come on now. How long do you think you'll be able to have your cake and eat it too? Just like I got tired Tia will too if you don't come off the bullshit."

"What do you care?"

"She's a good woman."

"Really, this coming from you?"

"Yes, this coming from me. I mean, no I didn't like her at first. I had every reason not to but I can't totally fault her for everything that went down and at this point I can't do nothing but thank her and you both."

"You want to thank me?"

"Yes, I thank you. Really, I do."

"Was I really that bad?"

"A lot worse than you think."

"You don't miss me, not even a little bit?"

"I miss the good times, the friendship but as far as missing us as a couple, we ran that course and what's done is done."

"But do you miss me?"

"Not in the way you want me to."

"Do you still love me?"

"I'll always love you Nathan for a whole lot of reasons but I don't love you the way you want me to anymore. I'm not in love with you and I am perfectly content with that."

"Pour me another shot" he said before getting up to let Anthony and Chyna in.

"Damn, y'all back here big kickin it" Anthony said as he came and grabbed some lounge chairs for him and Chyna.

Myangel passed him the bottle of Hennessy. Nathan came out with more cups and another bottle. Myangel made Anthony and Nathan both hand over their keys.

"Just like old times" Chyna said with a smile in Anthony's direction.

Nathan and Myangel both watched as the two kissed as if they were all alone, as if nothing had changed. Nathan took his seat back beside Myangel and passed Anthony a blunt.

Tia had gone off to bed on the other end of the house. Margaret had sat listening to the conversation between Myangel and Nathan. After Anthony and Chyna arrived the backyard got quiet.

"Y'all alright out here" Margaret asked as she stepped out onto the back porch.

"Yeah Ma, we're good. You want a drink" Nathan asked.

"No, I'm about to go to bed."

"Don't none of you even think about leaving this house" she said before turning and walking off.

They all laughed. "Some things never change" Myangel said with a smile.

"Yeah and some things do" Nathan said before taking the blunt from her hand without her passing it to him.

"Why you gotta be so damn rude" Myangel asked as she popped his arm.

"Why you gotta be so damn cute?"

"Oh I'm cute now? Earlier I was ugly."

"Didn't call you ugly. I said you had an ugly look on your face."

"Same thing" she said as she licked her tongue out at him.

It took everything in him not to go for her, wrap his arms around her and put his tongue deep in her mouth. Instead he leaned over and kissed her cheek.

"You win Mya" he said with a smile.

"I always do. Tell me something I don't know."

Anthony and Chyna took one of the kids old bedrooms while Nathan and Tia shared the guest bedroom. Myangel lay awake in her old bedroom on the phone with Dante' for the rest of the night and morning, falling asleep on the phone like teenagers.

"Aww ain't that cute" Margaret was saying the next morning when she noticed.

"Ain't what cute" Nathan asked when he walked into the room. He saw what his mom saw but his reaction was not the same, instead he frowned.

"Mommy, mommy, mommy" all the kids screamed out waking her up from a deep sleep. It wasn't long before they were in bed with her.

Gerrard had her cellphone up to his ear waking Dante' up who had also held the phone all night. Myangel wasn't ready to get up yet. She was hungry but had a hangover from all the Hennessy she drank the night before. Margaret figured they all could use some more sleep. She had invited Tia to hang out with her and the kids for the day. She felt that what Myangel had said last night made perfect sense. There were things Tia couldn't get used to if she was never around and people she would never really get to know if everybody didn't put forth the effort. This was said in front of the children, Nathan and Tia as well.

Myangel and Chyna were awake before Nathan and Anthony. They decided to have lunch at Flannigan's then go to the spa. Myangel extended the invite to Tia. She agreed to meet them at the spa but had already agreed to have lunch with the kids.

"I am so proud of you" Chyna told Myangel as they sat in a booth at Flannigan's.

"What? Why?"

"The way you're handling this whole situation with Tia and Nathan."

"I am so ready to move on with my life and I hate to admit that it took Gerrard to get me to understand that."

"Gerrard, what do you mean?"

Myangel explained to Chyna the conversation Gerrard had with Dante', the conversation she and Dante' had, the one she had with Gerrard and then the group conversation they all had together.

"I understand all this communication for the kids. But I mean damn, this nigga got another little boy the same age as the twins. That shit pisses even me off. Lying, cheating, good for nothing muthafuckas."

Myangel laughed, she couldn't help it. Chyna was right, Anthony and Nathan were both lying, cheating muthafuckas. She couldn't get with the 'good for nothing' because at one point Nathan was good for quite a few things. And seeing as how Chyna spent the night with Anthony, he obviously was still good for something too. Still it was something to laugh about.

"You know they've been talking about us right?"

"Anthony and Nathan, you mean?"

"Hell yeah, had the nerve to call us scandalous. These muthafuckas fucking Barbara, Jane, Betty, Sue and all they sisters and cousins."

"Not just fucking them, getting them pregnant too" Myangel had to laugh again.

"What's so damn funny? They don't care what that shit did to us. They don't care that they created a whole lot of drama for everybody involved. Fucked up relationships. Sorry bastards."

"Well damn C, you ran off with the nigga last night like none of this was relevant. What's up now?"

"I just hate the way everything went down. They played us."

"You could look at it that way."

"What other way do I have?"

"In reality they played themselves. I won't lie and say shit wasn't ugly, wasn't fucked up"

"You can't say that. Shit's real fucked up."

"Yeah but who's really getting the short end of the stick? I sure as hell ain't. I was doing my part. Yes I have 4 kids now but I'm still good. He got all these kids by all these different women, all this child support to pay, all these other headaches and it turns out he's not really as happy on the other side as he thought he would be. But you know what, I am. I'm happy for him, for me, for the kids, for everybody involved."

"Save that shit Myangel. You trying to be politically correct. I want to fuck them up."

"You don't think you're doing enough of that already"

"Shut up, if you wasn't so caught up on Dante' you would be fucking Nathan too."

"Thank God for Dante'" Myangel said as she took a sip of her drink with a big smile.

Dante' sent Myangel a text message. Although he was at work he kept the line of communication between them open. She always knew when she was on his mind and vice versa.

"What the hell you over there skinning and grinning about now?"

"That man, that man, that man"

Before leaving Flannigan's Chyna got a call from Anthony. She suddenly changed her plans and decided not to go to the spa. She invited Myangel to come along since Nathan would also be in tow but Myangel declined. Instead she went on ahead to the spa where she met up with Tia.

"Hey lady" Myangel said as she walked into the salon spa and greeted Tia. "How did everything go?"

"Those kids are a handful" she laughed with a bright smile. "I've never had all of them together at one time for so long but we had a really good time. We went to the mall to do a little shopping, spent quite a bit of time at the arcade and then to Luigi's for pizza and more games."

"Sounds like fun. Glad you enjoyed yourself. Come on here. Let's get pampered."

Myangel relaxed as her masseuse started working her magic. The massage coupled with the scent of Jasmine and the relaxing Neo soul music playing from the surround speakers made her completely relax. She was caught up in her own world fantasizing about what she would do to Dante' once she arrived back home. She had a pleasant smile on her face.

"Well damn, it's good but you act like you over there in orgasmic bliss" Tia told her with a laugh.

Myangel laughed too "Honey, if only you knew."

"What do you have planned after this?"

"I was just going to grab a bite to eat and go back to the house."

"Do you mind some company? I would like to talk to you about something."

"No, that's cool."

After enjoying time at the full service spa the ladies decided to stop by Wingstop to pick up some wings to go. Next stop was the liquor store. With the kids being away for the night with Margaret and Sal Myangel would enjoy some quiet time at home with good music, a good movie, a good book, a few drinks and a blunt or two.

"Make yourself comfortable. I'm going back here to put on my pajamas."

"Pajamas, this time of day?" It was barely 3 in the afternoon. The sun was shining bright and everybody and their mama was just getting out for the day.

"Yes, do you know how hard it is for me to get a moment like this" Myangel laughed.

"If you want me to come back another time, it's cool."

"No, you're good. Just give me a minute."

Myangel changed her clothes, grabbed Nathan's weed stash and made her way into the kitchen. She grabbed plates and glasses before making her way into the den area. Tia was trying to decide what to watch when Myangel suggested they watch Black Girls Rock that had been saved on the DVR. They each fixed a plate of wings, carrots and celery and poured Coconut Rum mixed with pineapple juice before sitting down to enjoy the show.

"So what's up" Myangel assumed Tia was just as into the show as she was when she didn't initiate the conversation she wanted to have. When Black Girls Rock got under way and several commercials had come and gone she couldn't wait any longer.

She noticed that Tia was kind of hesitant to say whatever needed to be said but she didn't want to have to ease it out of her. If it was at all important it would come out eventually. The doorbell rang. Anthony was dropping Chyna off so that he could go handle some business.

"What are you doing here" Chyna said when she walked in and set eyes on Tia.

"Chyna" Myangel said as she looked at her closely. "What is wrong with you?"

"Your brother gets on my everlasting nerve."

"And you come up in here giving attitude like we did it" Myangel said as she rolled her eyes and neck in true fashion.

"I'm sorry" she said as she looked over at Tia. She faced Myangel and asked "You accept my apology"

"Hell nah, but I'm sure we'll talk about it later. Here" she said as she passed her a blunt and got up to get another glass with ice.

"What y'all watching" Chyna asked Tia?

"Black Girls Rock" Tia passed Chyna the pineapple juice and Myangel passed her a plate.

Anthony text Myangel to call him. She kept seeing Chyna pick up her phone and drop it back in her lap several times. She figured he was trying to get a hold to her. She excused herself from the den and went into her bedroom. Before calling Anthony she tried Dante'. He didn't answer so she left him a sweet message telling him she wished he was there. She dialed Anthony.

"Yo sis, tell C to quit trippen. I'm coming back in a few hours. I ain't out here on bullshit, just trying to take care of some business. Straight up."

"Alright Anthony"

Dante' was calling on the other end. "What's up sexy Bebe" he asked with a smile in his voice.

"Nothing babe. What's up with you?"

"About to head to a briefing. Did your package come yet?"

"What package" she was asking when the doorbell rang. She made her way from the bedroom to the front door. She screamed when she opened it and saw him standing there. She jumped right into his arms and kissed all over his face.

Chyna and Tia were up out their seats when she started screaming and now standing in the foyer watching the two lovebirds go at it.

"I knew it wouldn't be too long before you got here" Chyna told Dante' with a smile when he and Myangel finally came up for air. She gave him a hug before making her way back into the den.

"Babe you remember Tia, right?"

Dante' stepped forward to shake Tia's hand. Myangel and Dante' made their way into the den. By the time Black Girls Rock was going off Chyna and Tia were comfortable and off to another show. Myangel and Dante' were headed to the master bedroom to steal intimate moments.

Chapter 17

They were wrapped up in each other's arms in bed when the alarm beeped alerting the opening of a door in the house. It wasn't long before Anthony and Nathan's loud mouths could be heard. They were fussing about the party starting without them.

"Where Mya" Anthony asked.

As awkward as the moment was Myangel didn't want to move out of the comfort of Dante's arms. Dante' didn't want to be at a disadvantage lying in bed if anything was to jump off. Without him saying those exact words she knew it was coming.

"Let's get up Bebe" he said as he waited for her to get up. He watched as she stepped into her pajamas making no move to leave the room. He walked over to her, wrapped his arms around her before kissing her lips. "Let's go face the music" he said as he took her hand.

Anthony was questioning Chyna about where Myangel was when she and Dante' walked from the back. The room went silent as Anthony and Nathan starred on without comment.

Myangel made introductions despite the angry look on Nathan's face and the confused look on Anthony's. She knew it would be a tad bit uncomfortable but a hump that they all needed to get over sooner rather than later.

Tia sat watching Nathan watch Myangel. Chyna watched Dante' and Nathan both. Anthony looked at his sister. Nobody said a word.

The silence was interrupted by the kids rushing in through the garage door calling out for "Mommy" They almost knocked her over trying to get in her arms.

When they saw Dante' every child but Nathaniel went after him. It wasn't long before they were all caught up in their own little world, as usual. Nathan's blood was boiling even more so now than it was when he realized Dante' was there. Sal and everyone else noticed. At the moment Dante' could care less.

Margaret and Sal initiated conversation with everyone in an attempt to lighten the mood. Margaret gave Myangel a big hug. "Our plan was to stay out all night but the kids wanted to come home."

"It's no problem Mom. There is plenty of room for everybody."

By now it's a little after 7pm. Myangel asked if the kids had eaten yet. Margaret said the plan was to order out but they hadn't agreed on what to eat just yet.

Game time was near. Sal suggested that the guys get out to do some male bonding. Chyna suggests that Myangel call Big Mike to meet up with them. Margaret agreed for various reasons. They ordered Chinese food for dinner.

Once all the men left the house and the kids were off doing their own things Margaret looked at Myangel and said "Baby I know you want everything to be cut and dry. I know you have been accepting of a lot of things and I know you've tried on so many levels for so many reasons."

Myangel knew there was a but coming. She knew it had to do with Nathan and how he felt about her having Dante' around. Never mind the fact that Tia was there, along with 2 children he fathered outside of their marriage. Never mind that the house was hers after the divorce and available for her to come home to whenever she felt the need or want to. It was all about Nathan and his feelings, always about how to make his world perfect. Never about how anyone else felt in any situation. It had been this way for so long that not very many people saw anything outside of his make believe perfection. The line had to be drawn somewhere. He had moved on with his life long before the ink dried on those divorce papers. Hell he was gone before then, truth be told. Now that she's truly moving on he wants to set boundaries and make demands. Shit ain't going down like that Myangel told herself. She didn't have to say anything. The look on her face said it all. Margaret bit her lip before walking off to join the kids. Chyna looked at Myangel with mixed emotions all over her face. Tia grabbed a blunt and

Myangel's glass and passed it to her before heading out to the back porch. Myangel said nothing as she followed.

"You alright" Tia asked Myangel a few minutes after sitting out back in total silence.

"I'm good. You alright?"

"Not really."

"What's wrong?"

"I feel like a total fool."

"Why?" Myangel asked as she looked at her.

"All this time I accused you of wanting Nathan back. I blamed you for damn near every argument we have."

"Yeah but we talked about that already. I don't want Nathan. I haven't wanted Nathan in years honey. Trust me, there is nothing he can do for me but stay out of my way as I move on." Myangel took the blunt Tia passed to her. She inhaled long and hard and let it out slowly a few times before sipping her Rum.

"I know and you sounded real sincere when you said it and I believed you. I guess I needed a reason to justify everything that has happened between Nathan and I, the arguments and fights."

"You don't have to justify anything Tia. Nathan is a certified asshole. I know this."

"I'm sorry for what I put you through. I'm sorry for coming in between the two of you."

Myangel laughed from the pit of her stomach. "Hell don't be sorry now. I promise you I'm so thankful. Don't get me wrong, it was hell at first. It was a bitter pill to swallow for sure. I gave that muthafucka everything I had in me" she said as she shook her head sadly. "It never was enough, at least not for him. As much pain as I was in knowing the circumstances then, I would go through it all again just to get to where I am now. This happy space, this place I'm in with Dante'. So don't be sorry honey. Hell I ain't" she said again with another laugh as she finally passed the blunt back.

Chyna came outside after playing around with the kids a while. She asked Myangel "You must have a death wish?"

Myangel laughed, she was seriously finding it all comical. When she thought about how much she catered to Nathan even after all the wrong he'd done she couldn't help but laugh even more.

"What's so damn funny?" Chyna asked

"All of this" she said as she swept her hands in the air. "Nathan and I haven't been together in years. I'm getting married in a few months, happily married I might add. My kids are happy as well. Why the fuck would I give a damn about what Nathan thinks about all this? Nathan got exactly what he wanted. No pun intended" she said as she nodded in Tia's direction.

"Okay and you said all that to say what? We all know what he did. We all know he still cares. We all know he gone act a plum damn fool too. I wouldn't be surprised if they're already going at it" Chyna told her.

"Dante' can handle his own, trust me. I'm sure neither Sal, Anthony or Big Mike are going to allow it to go down like that anyway."

"But you brought him here, of all places" Chyna whined.

Myangel's neck roll started up again as she finished off her drink and poured another. "You mean here, as in my house" she pointed. "That nigga don't run shit up in here no mo. He just thinks he does."

Chyna sat there shaking her head. It wasn't long before she got up from her seat and headed back into the house where she called Anthony to find out what was going on. Anthony told her that Nathan never left with them, that he took another route. Shortly after their telephone conversation ended Nathan was walking in through the front door.

He walked into the kitchen, the living area and the den before heading to the master bedroom. He pushed the door open smelled the sex in the air and got even *more pissed off than he was before. He checked the master bathroom before heading out to the back porch where he found Myangel and Tia sippin drinks and smoking a blunt together.*

"Myangel, let me holla at you for a minute" he said in a calm, even tone.

Tia automatically starts getting up. Myangel looks at her like she's crazy. Nathan looks at her like she better move quickly, and she does.

Myangel was knocking down drinks. She was pouring herself another one when Nathan asked her "Why the fuck you bring that nigga here?"

"You really gave up a night to bond with the fellas to come and ask me some shit like that" she asked as she gave him the screw face.

"Fuck that shit man, that don't have nothing to do with that nigga being here in our house, in our bed."

"Our" she asked incredulously. "Nigga, how easily you forget. This is my house. Everything in it belongs to me. Your 'our' is clear across town somewhere. Get the fuck on with that bullshit" she was saying just as Margaret came to the door to make sure everything was okay.

"Say, all bullshit aside, that nigga can't stay here."

"Nathan, all bullshit aside, go home."

Nathan started popping his knuckles and pacing back and forth as his Mom stepped outside to calm him down. Myangel put fire to the blunt that had gone out and ignored Nathan's rants. Chyna heard the commotion and immediately called Anthony. He was on his way.

By the time he arrived Nathan was arguing with his Mom who tried to convince him to go somewhere and calm down. Myangel got up from her porch swing and made her way into the house. As she passed the den Semaja came over and wrapped her arms around her. "I love you Mommy."

"I love you too baby."

"When is D coming back?"

"He went to watch the game with your Papa and Uncles."

"But is he coming back?"

"Yeah baby, he'll be back."

Myangel took a seat in the den along with Tia and the kids. They were all watching the show Jessie and eating their Chinese food with the surround sound extra loud. Myangel didn't know if that was their doing or one of the adults trying to drown out all the noise. It was doing its job for sure.

"Mommy I'm so glad D here" Gerrard tells her as he gives her a taste of his Orange chicken.

"Me too" Semaj says "Even if y'all have to leave tomorrow."

"They don't have to, that was just the plan when Mommy was here by herself. Right Mommy" Gerrard asked as he looked into her eyes.

"Yeah baby, that was the plan."

"So now that D is here can y'all both stay longer" Semaja asked.

"Yeah Mommy, I think y'all should stay longer too. D did say we all need a vacation. This can be like a vacation so we get to visit all our family" Semaj added.

"Mommy, can you stay longer? Please" Semaja asked as she lay her head on Myangel's shoulder with puppy dog eyes looking up at her.

"I'll discuss it with Dante' and see what he thinks"

"He's going to say yes if he knows we all want him to stay" Semaj announced.

Myangel laughed, "You're probably right babe"

By the time Dante' and Sal arrived back at the house Anthony, Chyna, Nathan and Tia were gone. The house was full of laughter as those remaining watched the movie Annie. The girls on the movie were singing 'It's a hard knock life'

When they realized Dante' was in the room it was like they never saw him earlier. Even Nathaniel was up from his seat this time. The adults looked on with smiles. Sal walked over and hugged Myangel. He never got around to earlier with all the commotion going on.

"You look wasted" he told her as he kissed her cheek.

She laughed "I'm good, buzzin a little."

"Margaret and I planned to stay here tonight, if that's okay with you."

"Always okay with me Pops" she smiled. "I so miss you guys"

Once all the kids were bathed and off to sleep Myangel and Dante' enjoyed a nice hot shower together. While lying in bed afterwards Myangel asked "How did you like the male bonding?"

"Not nearly as much as the bonding I'm about to get with you"

That was his way of saying he didn't want to talk about it. Myangel was not at all offended. Bonding is what they did for the next few hours. She never got around to mentioning that the kids wanted them to stay the entire Spring break in Miami. When the kids asked Dante' the next morning while Myangel still slept in bed his response was "I'll talk it over with your Mom and see what she thinks."

Gerrard told him "You know y'all both said the same thing, right."

Dante' laughed as he popped Gerrard on the back of the neck. He walked to the backroom after Sal and Margaret left to take the kids for breakfast at The Enchilada. He woke her up with his tongue on her clit.

"Now that's what the fuck I'm talking about" she said as she kissed his lips after her climax.

"You missed me, baby"

"Hell yeah"

Myangel fixed omelets and grits for breakfast and the two enjoyed breakfast in bed.

"You know Nathan probably plotting to kill you right?"

"He better suck that shit up" she laughed.

"You know the kids want us to stay longer, right?"

"Yeah they mentioned it last night. Do you need to rush back home? Are you comfortable staying here?"

"I'm straight Bebe. If you don't have no problem staying I'm cool." He watched her as she picked over her food. "What else is on your mind?"

"How I want to sop you up with a biscuit."

"You ain't got no biscuit" he laughed.

Chapter 18

Myangel and Dante' agreed to spend the rest of Spring Break in Miami. Once Nathan got wind of this he would call or text Myangel telling her how trifling she was. He even went so far as to say he was glad he fucked around on her, claiming that it lead him to meet a real woman. Myangel actually listened to him in a drunken stupor one night when he bragged about how much more of a woman Tia had been to him. He bragged about Tia not fucking around on him and how she should have been the one he married. Myangel was still laughing at it all because she knew even Nathan didn't believe the shit he was saying. Whether she hooked up with Dante' or not didn't change the fact that he wanted her back.

Dante' got tired of the phone calls and text messages. He wasn't jealous, just felt that Nathan was taking disrespect to a whole nother level. The night before they were to head back home to New York Dante' went out with the hope of somehow running into Nathan in the club or somewhere out on the block. He had every intention of stepping to him if the opportunity presented itself.

Nathan wasn't trying to get out at no club. He and Tia had been in to it every day since leaving Myangel's place. Although he talked about Tia being the better woman, the woman he wanted to be with; he was still fired up about Myangel being with Dante' in his face. What Tia had witnessed that day only confirmed the thoughts she had denied for so long. Nathan never stopped loving Myangel, in fact, he was still madly in love with Myangel. The crazy thing is that all this time she believed Myangel was the one interfering with her and Nathan's relationship, the reason why they couldn't advance. She had been wrong all along. All the excuses in the world couldn't justify the shit that was going on now. Tia was mad at herself for believing in him. She was even more pissed off to realize just how cool Myangel really was. She was literally slapping herself at the moment for a whole lot of reasons.

Once back home in New York Dante' received a call from an old friend he grew up with in high school. This friend was having a bachelor party in

Pennsylvania and wanted Dante' and Malik to come through. Dante' had asked his mom to keep the kids while he and Myangel made their way to Pennsylvania since she was invited to the bachelorette party.

This old friend George had been real heavy in the dope game a few years ago. Dante' wasn't surprised at all the niggas that came out to help him celebrate but he was surprised to see Marko down in the lobby of the hotel. Marko was talking to a group of young cats. When he noticed Dante' he excused himself to come over and speak

Dante' had heard all about the beef Nathan and Marko were in to. Myangel said she had no clue why because the two had been the best of friends since birth damn near. She had asked Nathan on more than one occasion when during conversations with the kids they mentioned seeing Uncle Mark. Nathan would then tell Myangel how he no longer fucked with "that nigga" as if Marko was just some nigga off the street. These two had started out from the bottom and had been through some heavy shit together. Myangel wanted to know what was going on but didn't want it to seem like she was all in Nathan's business.

"Wassup" Marko asked as he made his way in Dante's direction leaving Tia standing on the other side of the room.

"Ain't nothing" Dante' replied back. The two of them chopped it up a minute before realizing that they were going to the same bachelor party and discussed how far back they went with the groom George. Marko asked if Myangel would be attending the wedding. When Dante' told him yeah Marko had a smirk on his face. Dante' took note of it but didn't speak on it. They both made their way upstairs to the Presidential Suite for the party.

When Dante' mentioned running into Marko later that night once returning back to the room he and Myangel occupied she had a smirk on her face. She felt like she would now get the chance to get to the bottom of what was going on between Nathan and Marko. Dante' wondered what was up with all the smirking. Again he maintained his cool and didn't speak on it. Instead he and Myangel sexed each other to sleep.

"What the fuck you mean I can't go to the wedding? Why not? I didn't come all the way here to sit in a hotel room."

"You the one all the time talking about keeping shit on the hush. If you don't want everybody to find out what's up then you better find you something else to get into."

"What the fuck does that have to do with anything?"

"A lot."

"Nobody around here knows who I am so why would it matter?"

"Because it fucking matters. Look you can figure out something else to do or take your ass back home. The choice is yours. But what you ain't gone do is go to this wedding."

"You're serious?"

"As a heart attack."

"That's so fucked up."

"Nah what would really be fucked up is if shit got out. That would be fucked up, for real."

Seeing the look on her face he calmed down pulling her into his arms and kissing her forehead. "Why don't you hit up the mall or something? Go to a spa and get all dolled up. I won't stay too long at the reception and once it's over we can go kick it."

"How we gone go kick it if we need to keep things on the low?"

"We will go to some spot a little distance away."

"I still don't understand why we got to do this here."

"Do you trust me?"

She nodded her head yes. "Well then, respect what I'm saying and just relax. I ain't on no bullshit, for real."

Chapter 19

The arguments between Nathan and Tia had kicked off so bad that neither one of them were staying around each other for too long. Tia had gotten so heated during a few of the arguments that she started throwing punches or anything she could get her hands on around the house. Things were real ugly. At the moment Nathan was packing up his shit. Although he had agreed to let Tia come and live with him he was regretting it now because he didn't have a place to go to when shit got rough. He had no intention of putting her out on her ass even though at times that's what he really wanted to do. After all the hateful shit he had said to Myangel he still figured he could go kick it at their old house. Wasn't like anybody would be there anyway. When he went by the house he tried to enter in through the garage. When his garage door opener wouldn't work he figured Myangel had it locked from the inside since nobody would be there for long periods of time. He then tried the front door. His key wouldn't work. His first reaction was to call her going off. It didn't take him long to think it over seeing as he needed her help at the moment. It was her house and shit was so ugly between he and Tia that he knew leaving until he cooled down would be best. Otherwise he would end up locked up somewhere and he wasn't feeling that.

"Fuck" he said as he sat in his car trying to come up with a way to ask Myangel about staying at the house. His mom had been telling him to apologize but of course he wouldn't listen. He didn't want to apologize at all seeing as how he was still upset about Myangel and Dante' being together his apology would be a flat out lie. One minute Nathan would try to be cool with the situation and then he would think about how much he missed Myangel and the kids he'd get mad all over again. He sat in the car another 20 minutes before dialing Myangel's number.

"Hello" she answered in a pleasant voice. No matter how often Nathan called or text her cussin her out with his bullshit she still didn't stoop to his level. Sometimes Nathan thought he would feel better if she would at least argue back.

"Mya, you busy?"

"Not really. What's up?"

"I need to holla at you for a minute on some real shit."

"Okay" she said hoping this wasn't another one of his tantrums about how he was against her marrying Dante'.

He sat there contemplating how to say what he needed to say and avoid an argument. Before calling her thought he had it all figured out but no words would come to him at the moment.

"Nathan, what is it" she asked impatiently.

"When do you plan on bringing the kids home?"

She ignored his "home" comment because she knew he was only being stubborn. "I'm leaving out on Friday so I can spend a couple of weeks with Mom."

"Dante' cool with that?"

"Why wouldn't he be" she asked while she silently took note of him saying Dante's name.

"I don't know, just don't think I would be too cool with you being clear across town if you was my woman."

"Unh huh" she laughed.

"You need me to pick y'all up from the airport?"

"If you're not too busy that would be okay. I planned to call a cab but if you're willing to pick us up that'll work too."

"Alright, I can do that" he said as if he was about to end the call.

"Nathan, is that what you called me for?"

"Nah but we can discuss it when you get here."

"You sure?"

"Yeah."

"You sound like you got a lot on your mind."

"I do."

"And you're not fussin."

"And"

"Come on now, every time you call all you do is fuss."

"Well, I ain't fussin now."

"Which means something else is going on. So what is it?"

"It can wait. We need to have a sit down."

"A sit down? The last time we had a sit down things got ugly and a lot of secrets came out."

"Why you always in the past?"

Myangel took note of his voice, the calmness in it. She almost hated these moments, the moments when she wanted to make amends with Nathan thinking he was ready to as well. Then in the next breath he would be on some other shit. She wanted to believe this time was different but she also knew better.

"Okay Nathan. We will see you on Friday" she said as she reached for the airlines printout information. She gave him all the information he needed before ending the call.

"What's up" Dante' asked as he lay beside her.

"Nathan's picking us up from the airport."

"That's what he called for?"

"He tried to play like that was it but I doubt it. He sounded like he had something else on his mind but he wouldn't go into details. Said we would talk about it face to face."

Dante' snuggled into Myangel just as Gerrard came into the room. "D, can you come here for a minute? I want to ask you something."

"Alright son."

"What you got to ask him that you can't ask him in front of me?"

"It's man stuff Mommy, nothing you can get into" Gerrard said as he kissed her cheek.

Myangel looked from Gerrard to Dante' and back to Gerrard again before saying "well alright now." She marveled at the relationship Dante' had with her children.

Dante' kissed her lips before telling her "Get some rest Bebe. I'm about to go have a man to man with the fellas" he laughed as he dapped up Gerrard.

She laughed at them as they both walked out like the cool cats they were.

Marko called "Sis, when did you say y'all coming to Miami?"

"We will be there Friday. Why, what's up?"

"I want to talk to you about something."

"Alright, what is it?"

"How long you gone be in town?"

"A couple of weeks. Why Marko" she was asking as Dante' walked into the room.

"I need to run something by you. Get your opinion on something. Something important."

"Okay. I'll call you when I get there."

"Alright cool."

Dante' looked at her and asked "Ain't you supposed to be getting some rest?"

"Ain't Dante', ain't?"

He laughed as he starred into her eyes reminding himself that he had no reason not to trust Myangel.

She kissed his lips as she pulled him down into the bed with her. They went back to cuddling as they watched back to back episodes of Living Single.

"What was the man to man about?"

"Do I be all up in your woman to woman conversations?"

She laughed some more. "Oh is that how we playing it"

"Nah babe."

"So why won't you tell me? I thought we talk about everything."

"We do, always remember that. The kids will talk to you about it later. Don't tell them I told you, let them bring it up."

"Everything okay?"

"With me it is, we'll know if you are after the conversation."

"Damn, what does that mean?"

"Nothing Bebe, calm down. Nothing to worry about. I promise."

Chapter 20

Nathan was standing at the gate waiting on Myangel and the kids to come through the door. When he saw them his heart swelled. The kids ran over to him and he enveloped them in his arms. All he heard for a good 5-10 minutes was Daddy this and Daddy that. He opened his arms to hug Myangel. She could tell he was in a good mood. She accepted the hug he offered. He asked her about additional luggage. Since the kids had clothing at his house the only luggage she needed was her own in which she had in her hands. He took her luggage with one hand and held Jasara in his other as he lead the way to his car.

He asked about eating so they ended up at an arcade spot enjoying pizza. Myangel and Nathan sipped on a few beers as the kids played video games.

"So what's up" Myangel asked as she looked at Nathan. "What's going on with you?" She paused as she really took a good look at him. "You look like you haven't been sleeping. You got bags all under your eyes."

"Wow."

"Wow what?"

"I'm surprised you noticed."

"I don't know why, but that's irrelevant. What's going on?"

"Shit ain't going right with me and Tia." He waited for her to laugh in his face, to tell him I told you so. When she didn't say anything he continued on without looking at her. "Things ain't working out. I'm thinking it's best that I pack my shit and keep it moving."

"Really" she asked

"Yeah, no bullshit." He told her how the two had been arguing lately and how Tia was acting shady since the night back at Myangel's place.

"Well what do you expect Nathan" she asked as she forced him to look up at her.

"What do you mean?"

"All this time you had her thinking I was after you. You know damn well I don't want you back."

"You don't want me back" he asked as he reached across the table for her hand.

She allowed him to hold it for a minute before reminding him "No Nathan, I don't want you back. You had her thinking I want you but your actions back at the house clearly showed it was the other way around. She finally opened her eyes to see that."

"Yeah but I ain't fucked up about it. I mean, I ain't feeling her like that. No bullshit."

"Have you told her that?"

"We ain't sat down and talked about it in depth" he said as he felt her looking at him. "Damn" he laughed "yeah I said ain't. You know what I mean. We been arguing a lot lately so I told her I was gone move around for a minute. Put some space in between us for now. Until I can figure out what direction I want this to go in."

"You picked a fine time to try and figure that out, don't you think?"

"I know I went about everything all wrong. I mean I tried."

"You tried? Really Nathan? How can you say you're trying when you're not even over me?"

"Who said I wasn't over you?"

"Nathan you can't keep stringing people along and before you can move forward you will have to accept the fact that I have moved on. You can't go into a relationship knowing that you're still in love with someone else. It will never work."

"On some real shit, I don't want to accept that you moved on. I don't want to accept that you're with Dante', that you moved to New York, that you talking about getting married. I don't want to accept none of that shit."

"But Nathan, you have to. It would make things a whole lot easier for the rest of us."

"Easy for who? Shit won't be easy for me. I still gotta live with that shit every day."

"You should have thought about that before you did what you did."

Nathan scooped Jasara up in his arms kissing her cheeks. She was finally adjusting to him. "You're right boo" he said to Myangel without looking at her. "You're right about everything. I should have thought about that shit a long time ago. Look I was fucking up and not taking shit seriously, not appreciating what I had at home and I just let shit get out of hand. Too out of hand."

As bad as Myangel wanted to throw out a few words of her own she held her tongue and listened to what sounded like a sincere apology or at least admission that he had done something wrong. She couldn't help but wonder what brought this on. She couldn't blame it on his arguments with Tia, the two of them argue all the time. It was nothing new.

"Look Mya, I'm sorry. I'm sorry for everything I put you through, all I put the kids through, the family. The shit I did was beyond fucked up."

The kids came running up for more pizza and drinks. It had been a good 2 hours since they arrived. Nathan and Myangel both agreed it was time to leave. When they arrived at the house Myangel unlocked the door and ran in to disarm the alarm. Nathan assisted her with getting the kids all settled in. This time when he got comfortable she didn't protest. She sensed that there was more he wanted to talk about. She offered him a beer and told him to get comfortable while she walked into her bedroom closing the door behind her. She phoned Dante' before starting her shower water. She told Dante' that Nathan was still there, what the two of them had discussed. She told him she was about to shower and get comfortable and would call him back later. Dante' told her he was cool.

Once she was fresh and clean she walked around the house. Everybody was in the den. When she walked in they got quiet. She looked around into the faces of her children and Nathan before asking "What's going on?"

Gerrard and Semaj had a sad look on their face. Nathan looked pissed. Again she looked around at everybody. Before her shower everyone had been happy go lucky.

Semaja said "Mommy we was thinking, you know, me and my brothers" she said as she used her hand motions.

"Semaja baby, you don't have to talk with your hands. What is it baby? What were y'all thinking" she asked as she looked into the eyes of her oldest children.

She knew Semaja would continue the conversation. She was the most outspoken one at any given time.

"Okay so Mommy, we was wondering if we could call Dante' Daddy too. You know since we're around him all the time and you're about to get married. And we just want to know."

Again Myangel looked at her kids and then the expression on Nathan's face. He was damn near in tears and a part of her felt sorry for him. She took a seat while taking a deep breath. "I wasn't expecting that" she confessed. She looked over at Nathan who had his head in his hands. To her children she said "Daddy and I need to talk. G, can you keep an eye on everybody, please?"

"Yes Mommy" he said as he took the hands of his sisters and told his brother to follow him.

Myangel walked over to the wet bar to grab glasses, a bottle of Hennessy and the weed stash before motioning for Nathan to follow her out to the patio.

"Do you think they're going to argue now" Semaja asked her older brothers.

"Daddy looked really mad" Semaj added in.

"Not really mad, just a little bothered by it" Gerrard added.

"A little, really" Semaja asked with her hands on her hips. "Are you kidding me? Daddy looked like he wanted to cry. He's more than a little bothered by it, trust me."

Gerrard and Semaj both laughed. "You know you sound just like Mommy, right?" Gerrard asked as he pushed her a little.

"So what, I'm for real though. What do you think they're going to say?"

"They're not arguing, otherwise it would be loud already. I don't hear anything, do you?" Semaj asked as he leaned closer to the closed door to see if he could hear anything.

"I don't hear nothing" Semaja told them. "That's a good sign."

Myangel passed Nathan the stash and watched as he rolled a blunt. She poured them drinks and looked out at the sky.

"Man" he said aloud as he fired up the blunt. "I can't believe they asked me that shit. I can't believe you didn't know. They usually talk to you about everything."

"I know, right" Myangel said as she thought back to the man to man conversation with Gerrard and Dante' and how Dante' said the kids would talk to her about it.

"I don't even know what to say. I mean I want to be mad, hell I am mad but I'm trying to see shit for what it really is. You know fully accept the consequences of my actions."

Myangel sipped her drink and took the blunt Nathan passed to her. Again she decided to listen rather than comment.

"I had something I wanted to talk to you about, now man I don't even" Nathan watched as Myangel smoked the blunt.

"What did you want to talk about Nathan?"

"I told you about all the shit that's been going down with me and Tia. I'm trying to accept responsibility for my actions and if I'm honest with myself I think I *just need some time to myself. I can't lie and say I'm over you. I can't keep trying to convince myself that I'm not the reason everything is going the way it's going. In all honesty I was feeling Tia but I was never feeling her on the level that I was feeling you. We was cool and all but we were never there, you know, where you and me was. I fucked all that up to get here and I ain't happy. I ain't happy at all. Yeah you might say it took you saying you're about to get married for all this to come out but that ain't it at all. I just been gassing myself up all this time. Thinking I had the winning hand but shit I ain't winning. The woman of my dreams is wrapped up in some other niggas arms every night. The woman I love is about to get married to some other nigga. All that shit about having you take a blood test with Jasara was bullshit. I never believed she wasn't mine, even after finding out about you being with Dante'. I just wasn't feeling him being in the picture and I wanted to get back at you. I wanted you to feel some kind of way about me asking you to have a blood test. I gave y'all hell in hopes that I could make you come back to me, or at least in hopes that you would stop fucking with the nigga."*

The two continued to pass the blunt between them and sipped on their drinks.

"The bottom line in all this is that I had the opportunity to make and keep you happy. I had plenty of chances to get it right and I just kept fucking up. I could have did better but I was trying to act like I was the man. Hell I thought I was the man, but that's bullshit and it took all this" he said as he swept his hand in the air *"all this for me to figure that shit out."*

"So what does all this mean?"

"It means that I'm trying to be a man, trying to admit my faults and move forward. If I'm honest with myself, I know shits been over with me and Tia. I've just been stringing her along and that shit ain't cool at all. Now I just gotta tell her and I don't know how she gone take this shit. I been lying to her and myself all this time. I think she gone go crazy for real and I almost don't want to tell her but I know I need her."

"Yeah you gotta tell her. You just have to be straight up with her yo. Don't keep filling her head up with bullshit. Just keep it real with her."

The alarm sounded and Margaret could be heard asking "Hey, where everybody at?"

Myangel and Nathan came from the back porch and joined the kids as they welcomed Grandma.

"Everything okay" she asked when she looked closely at Nathan.

Jasara was in Margaret's arms. Nathan leaned over and kissed her cheeks before kissing his mother's cheeks. "Nah" he responded "but it will be."

Myangel put Jasara to bed before checking on the kids who were still awake watching Pitch Perfect. She went into her bedroom and immediately dialed Dante'.

Nathan and Margaret sat out on the back porch discussing much of what Nathan had already discussed with Myangel but more in depth. The things he held back on expressing to Myangel he openly discussed with his mom. He even brought up the topic of staying in Myangel's house until he figured out exactly what he wanted to do with his life. He also told her he was considering walking Myangel down the aisle.

"I mean, there's nothing I can do to undo what I've already done. I just want to move forward without all that shit eating me up and I want me and Mya to be friends again."

"You miss her, don't you?"

"Yeah. Hell yeah. More than I ever thought I would."

"But you can admit it, and you're willing to admit it. That's the first step in the right direction."

"I just don't know how we can get back to that place. You know, where we was all close and shit. I used to talk to Mya about everything and she used to talk to me."

"The two of you talk sometimes."

"Sometimes Ma, I'm not feeling the sometimes."

"Well you do know she's about to get married, right? She will be someone else's wife."

"Yeah, I know all that and I ain't trying to interfere."

"Every time you start fussin and cussin when things don't go your way, when you try to act like you don't deserve any of this; that's interfering."

"I know Ma."

"Son, I'm going to be downright honest with you. Things will never go back to the way they used to be" Nathan sighed loudly, he knew this was the truth but he was accepting it in small doses.

"You have to earn her trust, her friendship, her respect. You took all that away with all that you had going on before. Don't be surprised if she questions how sincere you are in your approach. I mean here it is she's moving on, you and Tia aren't working out and you want to move back into the house. All this at once, just out of the blue."

"I know Ma but I ain't trying to bullshit around no mo. Yeah shit's fucked up with me and Tia and yes Myangel is moving on. I wish I could go back and start all over but I know I can't. But the truth of the matter is I ain't feeling Tia and shits so bad that I need to get away before it gets a whole lot worse."

"What is going on son? There is something you're not telling me."

Myangel stepped out onto the back porch and asked "Y'all alright out here?"

I see we trading places Margaret laughed since she's usually the one saying that to them. "Yeah we're alright. Here, come on out here and have a seat. The kids asleep?"

"Semaj and Jasara are but Gerrard and Semaja are watching Wreck It Ralph" she said as she took the seat Margaret and Nathan created in between them.

There was a long pause before Nathan poured Myangel a glass of Hennessy and passed it to her. She looked at him closely. "Alright now, what's really going on?"

"What you mean" Nathan asked.

"What you mean what I mean? Don't give me that nonsense Nathan Brooks."

He smiled at her, leaned over and kissed her cheek before telling her "I need to move back into the house. I don't know for how long."

"Okay, I knew this was coming" she said without attitude "I was going to suggest that anyway, I mean, if you wanted to, if you needed to. But that doesn't explain what's going on."

Margaret would normally get up and allow the two of them to discuss their issues in private but she sensed that this was a family discussion. A lot seemed to be weighing heavily on Nathan's mind. She, like Myangel, waited for him to open up. It took a lot for Nathan to open up the way he did.

Myangel heard her cell phone ringing inside. Thinking it might be Dante' she rushed into the house.

"Damn, she gone break her neck trying to get at that nigga" Nathan commented.

Margaret laughed, she knew he was only saying that out of jealousy. Inside Myangel was surprised to see Tia's name on the caller ID.

"Hello" she answered.

"Hey Myangel, I was wondering if you have some free time to get together for coffee tomorrow."

"Yeah that's cool. Everything okay?"

"I want to talk to you about something, you know what I mentioned before but never got around to discussing."

"Okay, what time works for you?"

"We could meet like say 11 or so."

"That works for me. Call me in the morning to confirm details. Now you sure everything is alright?"

"Yeah"

After she hung up with Tia she read her missed text messages. Marko had text her reminding her that she was supposed to meet him for lunch at 2. She replied back I haven't forgotten about it bro, dang. This had better be good too. Lol☺

"Y'all straight" Nathan asked as Myangel came back outside and took her seat.

"Yeah we good, now what's up with you? I ain't forget."

"I want to walk you down the aisle, if the option is still open."

"Really" she asked in disbelief. "The shit must have really hit the fan. Huh ma?"

Margaret laughed lightly before Nathan continued. "I want to walk you down the aisle, give you away to Dante'. I want to make amends with both you and him. I know it won't be easily accepted seeing as how I've made a complete mess of everything but I know it's for the best. I just need the opportunity to right my wrongs. I owe you and the kids that much."

Myangel accepted Nathan's apology in sincerity. In the back of her mind she still questioned why and wondered when the real reason would all come out. Nathan was only giving so much at the moment. She took the Hennessy bottle out of his hand and poured her another glass while seriously taking it all in. She told herself she probably couldn't deal with the reason why it was all coming out now.

Nathan didn't leave that night but was gone before Myangel got out of bed the next morning. Myangel woke up to the kids on the bed with her while they passed the phone back and forth between them while speaking to Dante'.

"Mommy is sleeping beauty" Semaja smiled as she kissed Myangel's cheek. "Good morning Mommy" she said when she slowly opened her eyes.

"Good morning babies" she said as she kissed and hugged each one and accepted the phone Semaj put into her hand. Dante' was wide awake and singing Babyface's Sunshine. Myangel couldn't do nothing but smile.

Just as Myangel was on her way out the door Tia called to cancel their meeting time for coffee. Myangel noted that Nathan must have been home and must have told Tia his big news because they were in the middle of a very heated argument. Myangel was trying to rush Tia off the phone so she wouldn't be in the middle of their business. She dialed Marko up to see if they could meet earlier. Marko agreed to and suggested Razzoo's as the meeting spot. Myangel was game and was really in the mood for their stuffed fish and a drink or two.

Marko stepped up in the spot looking all suave and debonair as usual. He wrapped his arms around Myangel practically lifting her off her feet as he hugged her close and kissed her cheeks.

"Damn sis, it's been a long time. How you been? You looking good than a muthafucka but that ain't nothing new. I guess marriage life is for some people."

"Yeah only the strong" she said as she popped his arm. "How are you?"

"I'm straight. Taking life one day at a time, you know how I do."

After placing their orders they talked about the kids, about New York and life with Dante'. Marko talked about how everything went down between Myangel and Nathan. He told her his outlook on things and how even in the back of his mind he still wished things had worked out between the two of them.

"You were the best thing that ever happened to him. He was just too damn blind to see it."

"I agree Marko, but for real, what's up with you two?"

Marko shrugged his shoulders and sipped his Heineken. Myangel looked at him and said "Come on now, don't shrug your shoulders at me."

"Shit got real."

"I can see that. You two were practically joined at the hip since we hooked up and were closer than close. So really, what the hell going on with y'all?"

Marko ordered another drink. They were still waiting on their food to come out. He ignored her question altogether and quickly tried to change the subject. Myangel was giving the waitress time to clear out because she had no intention of leaving the restaurant without finding out what went on.

"So when's the wedding date?"

Myangel smirked at him. "You ain't slick nigga. Stop playing."

"I'm for real, when's the wedding date Ma?" The expression on Marko's face changed from a smile to a mug. Myangel looked over her shoulder to see what he was looking at. Tia walked to the other side of the room hand and hand with a dude that looked vaguely familiar. A part of Myangel wanted to get up and be nosey but the grown up part of her reminded her that it was not her business. She had no ties to Tia other than sharing their baby daddy. What she did was her business, besides Nathan was ready for a break anyway. She returned her attention to her own table just as the waitress arrived with their food.

As soon as she walked off Marko shook his head. "You see that shit. That bitch trifling than a muthafucka" he said in a heated tone. "She fuck any nigga with long paper in his pockets."

"Damn, why you all salty about it" Myangel joked. Myangel was cracking more jokes when the frown on Marko's face deepened. Myangel looked over her shoulder again but didn't see anything so she assumed he was only referencing the same situation with Tia. That was until she heard a commotion from the other side of the room and what sounded like Nathan's voice accusing Tia of cheating on him. There were heated words exchanged between Nathan and Tia in the beginning. The dude with Tia wasn't smart enough to keep his mouth closed so he and Nathan started arguing. Marko was up out of his seat and Myangel was following close behind him. When Nathan saw the two of them walk up together he saw RED.

"What the fuck" he asked as he gave them both the screw face. To Marko he asked "Oh, let me guess, you fucking her too now?"

"Nathan" Myangel said as she looked at him with a look that cut him down in size.

"I'm saying though, what the fuck you doing with this nigga?"

"Why the fuck are you questioning me, first of all? And I don't know what trifling bitches you been dealing with that fuck your friends but that ain't me. You better get your mind right" she told him as she stood in his face giving off the same attitude he'd given her before. He turned around and walked out the restaurant. Myangel followed close behind him.

"What the fuck is going on" she asked as she tried to stop him.

"Nothing, I'll holla at you later."

Marko stepped outside, to Nathan he said *"Yo, chill out bro. No need in getting locked up over no bullshit."*

Nathan looked at Marko and shook his head. Myangel saw the look in his eyes, there was pain and regret. *"I ain't fucked up about it"* he told him. *"You did try to warn me. You tried to warn me about a lot of shit."*

"Where are you going" Myangel asked him as he hit the keypad to unlock the doors of his truck.

"I don't know. I guess I'll ride around for a bit."

"I'm riding with you" she told him, sensing that he was about to do something stupid.

"Y'all hit me up later, be safe" Marko told them as he fired up a Black & Mild and stood outside the restaurant.

Chapter 21

Myangel and Nathan ended up back at the house. Margaret had taken the kids to the airport with her to pick up Salvador and they had plans for the remainder of the day.

"You alright" Myangel asked Nathan as he sat at the bar with no drink starring off into space. Her cellphone rang, Dante' was calling to find out how her day was going. She spoke with him a good 45 minutes before someone came into his office.

Myangel was hungry. She never got to eat her food back at the restaurant and was a little upset about that but she sensed that Nathan really needed a friend right now. As he sat at the bar she fixed him a shot of Tequila and pineapple juice and passed him a rolled blunt before taking out the ingredients for chicken and steak fajitas. By the time she was turning off the burners on the food her cell was ringing again, she assumed it was Dante' calling her back.

Instead it was Tia. Tia seemed desperate to talk to her now. Myangel left the kitchen and made her way into the bedroom. She had to let Tia know that Nathan was at the house so she wouldn't come over.

"I told him" was all Tia kept saying. "I told him, I had to. I'm tired of living a lie."

"Okay" Myangel said not knowing exactly what she had told him.

"I told him I was seeing someone else, that I was leaving him to be with someone else."

"Wow" Myangel said as she took a seat on the bed.

"He didn't even care. I expected him to cuss me out, to try to fight me, to try and talk me out of it. He told me he's happy for me" Tia sobbed. "That bastard had the nerve to tell me he planned on leaving anyway, that shit just wasn't

working out between us. After all this time, after all the shit I been through in behind him and this nigga leaving me with no remorse."

Myangel heard the doorbell ring, when she walked out the bedroom Nathan was at the door letting Marko in. She returned to the bedroom closing the door behind her.

"He was packing his shit, packing his shit without a care in the world. Told me he'd call to schedule time to pick up Mioshi, said he'd already been down to the court to put himself on child support. He told me I could keep the condo, that he was moving out and that it was for the best."

"Okay but if you're moving on with someone else, why does it matter that he's moving out? I mean, shit that just makes it an easier transition for the both of you. You wanted out and he wanted out, what's the big deal?"

"What's the big deal? The big deal is that Nathan thinks he can treat people like shit and get away with it. He fucks up lives and goes about his business like nothing ever happened. I know you over him and you're with Dante' now but I remember how fucked up you were. I know how fucked up I feel right now and I just, I just want him to feel pain. I want him to hurt. I want him to want to kill himself in behind this shit. So I told him. I told him. I had to. I've been holding the shit in for too long."

Myangel sensed that there was more to it than just Tia seeing someone else. "What did you tell him, Tia?"

"I, I, I told him Mioshi ain't his."

Myangel gasped, it was true that she too had wanted Nathan to feel some kind of pain when she first learned he was cheating but never in a million years had she stooped to lying about the twins not being his. She was sure of them. She may not have been 100% sure about Jasara given the circumstances but she was sure about the twins. It hurt her to tell him that there was a slight chance Jasara was not his, even after all he did she didn't want to hurt him.

"It's true. Mioshi is not his baby."

"Now Tia, I understand what you're going through, no doubt. It's not that serious though."

"Myangel, you don't understand. I told him Mioshi wasn't his. I tried to explain but he didn't want to listen. He wouldn't let me finish. Mioshi is not his baby. I was messing around with practically all of them at the time"

"All of who" Myangel asked as she frowned up.

"All. Of. Them" Tia stressed.

"Oh shit" Myangel said having already figured it out long before she said it. Tia didn't have to explain any further. If Mioshi wasn't Nathan's child despite looking just like the twins and Jasara, there was only one other person she knew of that could be her father for sure. She had questioned the number of distinct features the two shared for as long as she could remember. Every time she brought up the subject nobody took her seriously.

"Mioshi is Marko's baby. He doesn't know it. Nobody knows it but you and me. I tried to tell Nathan, really I did. I tried but he wouldn't listen."

"Why, why would you carry on all this time knowing the truth?"

"Because Marko told me from day one I was just a piece of ass. That's all I ever was to him."

"And Nathan, he told you what?"

"Nothing, nothing until I told him I was pregnant. Then he started to see a future for us."

"Or he just tried to accept his responsibility" Myangel said as she shook her head. "You have to tell them the truth."

"I tried. Nathan won't listen and Marko hasn't said more than two words to me since he found out I was more than just a fuck to Nathan. When Nathan and I were just fucking it was cool because they share randoms all the time. But shit got fucked up when I told him I was having Nathan's baby. Marko tried to tell Nathan he was trippin trying to turn a hoe into a housewife. Marko was so convinced he'd always strapped up that he never even considered Mioshi being his. The minute I started fucking them I poked holes throughout all the condoms. I never took birth control. I was trying desperately to get pregnant. I wanted to be taken care of the way that Nathan was taking care of you. That's all I wanted and having a baby was the only way I could get it. I did what I had to do."

"And why exactly are you telling me?"

"I'm telling you because I know you're the only one that can get to Nathan. He'll listen to you. He'll believe you."

"Why would he believe me on some shit like this?"

"I tried to get pregnant by Nathan but it never happened. We stopped using condoms, I still wasn't using birth control. It just wouldn't happen."

"You tried to have another baby so you could really hold on to him, huh" Myangel said as she left the bedroom and set out to find Nathan and Marko. She wasn't surprised that the two of them were sitting out on the patio smoking a blunt and sippin on drinks. When they noticed her she was able to take the seat in between them, motioning for them to be quiet she put her phone on speaker.

To Tia she asked "What do you want me to do with all this" before putting her phone on mute.

"I need you to tell Nathan that Mioshi is not his baby. He needs to know the truth." Tia laughed wickedly. "Tell him that Mioshi is Marko's baby. Tell him if he doesn't believe me he should call Dr. Manuel's office to be sure. When he asked for a blood test for Jasara I paid a nurse to perform one on Mioshi. She's not his. She's Marko's baby, deep down I've always known this. I was getting what I always wanted and everything was going great until he told me he was leaving me, until he showed me he never gave a damn about me. Then I had to make him hurt. I had to tell him."

Both Nathan and Marko sat there with shock written all over their face. Nathan looked at Myangel, starred deep into her eyes now seriously giving thought to all that he lost. Marko sat on the other side of her "Ain't this about a bitch" he said as he got up and walked off.

EPILOGUE

Six months later, Myangel was dressed in an all white dress and being escorted down the aisle by Nathan. Everything had worked itself out. Nathan had dealt with the fact that she had moved on, and even became cordial with Dante'. Everyone was enjoying the wedding and reception. Nathan made his exit just moments before Myangel and Dante were about to head out for their honeymoon. He sat in his car directly in front of the pearl white limousine; he smoked his blunt as tears rolled down his face. Nathan had stood strong, but was really broken inside. Giving Myangel away took a toll on him, but making her happy was well worth it. It took him back to the time when he first started getting to know her and Gerrard. That thought alone was worth a lifetime. Looking up he saw Myangel exiting the church with Dante' on her heels. They both were full of smiles as a small crowd followed close behind them. Nathan wore an evil grin as he rubbed his fingers across the nine millimeter in his lap. He wasn't going to let the day go as planned. Nathan had just the move to make her really think about everything they shared. Before Myangel and Dante' were able to make it inside the limousine the sound of a gunshot was heard. Everyone ran for cover.

Myangel looked up and noticed Nathan sitting in his car with blood everywhere.

When she approached the car, she saw Nathan's breathless body, with an envelope addressed to her. She wasted no time opening it up.

Mya. You will always be my love. I have learned so much about life from you. These streets are not for me. It's been a hell of a ride. One neither of us could ever forget. I did as you wished, walked you down that aisle. That was the hardest thing I ever had to do in my life. So hard that I just want to kill myself. I must have done it already if you are reading this letter. I'll keep it simple because you have a honeymoon to attend. Now you will have two reasons to remember this day. The day you married that nigga, and the day you killed me mentally and emotionally. Yeah you may not have pulled the trigger, but your actions pushed me here.

The Ultimate Wheelchair Hustla

By Michael Conliffe

INTRO

It was all good just a week ago, Dusty was saying to himself, as he layed out in this coffin, with all his family, and friends mourning his death. The more he glanced out at the crowd the more he said "Damn, I knew my time was coming. What a hell of a ride it was though. I hope Mike stands strong through this, and keep the family straight, he got my little niece to look after." As Dusty continued to scan the crowd, he got a look at his parents trying to hold it strong, all he could think to himself was "DAMN, I fucked the family up! I been knew I should have stopped! I should have went to the Olympics when that offer was there, but instead I choose to do this. What the fuck was I thinking?" As those thoughts were going through his head, he was listening to a familiar voice talking about him, but for some strange reason Dusty couldn't take his eye's off his family. The more he stared at his family, and the more he heard the voice, he realized exactly who it was talking. It was Allen's father talking. That put a little smirk on Dusty's face for a minute, because he never heard him say so much at one time in his life. Allen's father was saying "Dusty use to come to my house all the time! Crawling up the stairs, not wanting no-one to help him, and we had a dog named Liberty that use to love when he came over there, because he would bite at his pants making them come down every time he went up the stairs. Between Dusty, Michael, and Allen, you never knew what type of trouble they had in store for you. They were so sneaky, you wouldn't have even expected them to have done that." As the smirk grew wider, he saw the only person that he wanted to look up to him standing up moving his way from the front row of the church to the back door with tears flowing out his eyes like waterfalls. At that moment the smirk must have left his face, because the entire morale of the church changed, and that alone made the reality of his death take more of a toll on everyone, than it had already done. As Dusty watched Mike exit the door, he sent word to the only ones worth sending word to, THEIR IMMEDIATE CIRCLE OF FRIENDS/FAMILY WHO KNEW EVERYTHING ABOUT EACH OTHER!

As Dusty spoke with Big Stan, Adam, Drew, Daron, and Allen, telling them to go check on Mike from his coffin, he watched one of the other cousins go out after Mike to console him. Dusty started mumbling to himself "Get your clown ass out of here. Niggaz ain't feeling you. When we actually tried to talk with you on some money investment shit, you played us to the left, like we were broke, with yo broke ass."

The guys must have got the message, because at one particular moment, they all headed out the church at one time, heading to check on Mike. Mike was going crazy, crying like a baby, feeling alone in the world, and out of nowhere he felt like Dusty was speaking to him saying "I am always going to be here for you, just listen when I speak, and be conscious of the ones I send at you. They are at your aide and assistance out of love, and respect." Once the voice faded, a circle approached, each and everyone knowing how Mike felt at the time, because they all were hurting in their own way. They slowly pushed David out of the way, and Stan, and Daron put their arms around his neck. I guess that was the time for everyone to speak, because they each basically said the same thing, saying "You are not alone, you got brothers in all of us, and we are here for you like we were Dusty, now come on back inside, and let's make sure Dusty get's sent off in style."

Let's do a recap to what lead up to this here so you won't be lost, and have a further understanding about Dusty!

Chapter 1

"Dusty can't do that with ya'll get from round here, he's undeveloped" Dusties great grandfather use to say to all of his cousins, when it came time to playing piggy in the back yard, but what should you have expected? His great grandfather came from a totally different generation, but regardless to what Mr. Dave (that's what he called his great grandfather) said, Dusty always found his way to play piggy. "Dusty you up at bat" his cousin Elkey would always say, letting him get the first go around. Each and every time Mr. Dave would say that, he would watch out of the window, knowing his grandson was setting out to beat the odds, and this time was just like all the others, Dusty had made him proud once again, by not letting his handicap stop him. Dusty was born with Spina Bifida, making him live his life in a wheelchair. That didn't mean squat in his family though, because he had the type of parents that wasn't allowing him to use his handicap as a crutch. They kept him involved in sports. He was playing wheelchair basketball since he was 6 years old, and in track, competing against other handicapped kids. With him being able to do all that, why should he be allowed to use his handicap as a crutch? Shit, he was doing more than people without a handicap.

Each and every Saturday morning you would hear "Dusty, Michael, get up and clean these bathrooms, and scrub them floors. Once you are done with that, cut the grass, and dusty take this screwdriver out to the driveway, and pull them weeds' their father would say to his two sons. Like always Dusty found a way to manipulate Mike into doing the majority of the work, by being slick with word play, and using that older brother tactic on the younger one. By noon, Dusty would be done doing his part of the cleaning, and now trying to stay out of dodge, so he wouldn't be thrown anymore work to do. Dusty would catch his father off guard like clock work saying "Dad, you want to play some cards?" He realized that if he got his father playing cards for about an hour, he wouldn't have no more work to do afterwards.

Now school was another thing. Dusty stayed getting good grades, was cool with just about everyone, and in elementary school he held the record for pull-ups in his 6th grade year. He did something like 30 pull-ups. Yeah we are saying that's nothing now, but for a 6th grader, that's a hell of a number. You got to realize how strong he had to be, to push himself his entire life in a wheelchair, no power chair, just manual pushing. Well as time went on, the school decided to have a fund raiser, where the kids collect money for jump rope for heart, or sell candy to win prizes. This was the time Dusty was waiting for. He realized that everyone would buy the candy from him, because he is in a wheelchair, and if they wouldn't buy it from him, he had Mike, his younger brother who was 3 years younger than him, whom they probably buy it from. When Dusty made it home from school, he yelled "Mike, come here." Mike came, and Dusty started running his game on him, teaching him at the same time. He said "Mike, you got one of these catalogs too don't you?" Mike shook his head yeah, then dusty continued on. He then said

"You know the people buy this candy from you, and when you take it to the school in 3 weeks they give you the candy for you to give to the people don't you?" Again Mike shook his head yeah, but the entire time looking at the prizes he could win if he sold a lot of candy, so he wasn't focused on what Dusty was saying. Dusty continued "Well we are going to sell everyone the candy, and keep the money, so we can buy us some more games for our Nintendo, and then we going to buy us some candy and sell at school." Mike looked up at Dusty and asked the stupidest question, and that was "can I ask mommy to buy some candy, because I want to win that bike?" At that moment I think Mike finally realized that Dusty could beat his ass, because Dusty punched Mike dead in the chest, making him cry, then putting a pillow over his head saying "You better be quiet, because if they hear you crying, we both going to get into trouble."

Well Mike finally understood the plan, and Dusty and him hit the streets selling candy, going door to door. As they collected the money, their eyes kept getting bigger, and when people payed with checks, they would just put that with the rest of the money, and figure out what to do with them later. After a few days of doing it Dusty counted the money up and said "Mike, we got about $40.00, and these checks. Tear them up, and throw them in the garbage, but make sure you put them at the bottom so no-one can see them", and that's exactly what Mike did. The next day was the day to turn in the paperwork for all the candy that was sold, and Dusty told his teacher he didn't sell any, as she skipped right on over him, as he looked at all the other suckers who turned their orders in. That weekend, Dusty and Mike got a ride to Toys R Us to go buy a new video game, and when their parents asked them "where did ya'll get the money from to buy this game from?" Dusty replied quick saying "We been saving our money, and lunch money too." The rest of the money they had, they went to buy some candy wholesale from the distributor. Dusty talked his mother into taking them up there to get some, which she agreed to do. Since they had candy now, and was in two different grades, they started selling it at school to all their friends, getting all their lunch money, and after school money. At first they were not making much money, but over time they started bringing home about $15.00 a day from candy, and as they got older and went to different grades the money kept growing.

By the time Dusty made it to high school, he decided to quit selling candy, and start scheming on peoples kindness. He purchased him a car when he was 16, and got him some hand controls to attach to the brake/accelerator, so he could be able to drive, and off he was. He observed how his wheelchair basketball team had them selling candy in front of stores to help support them in their travels, and that people were actually just giving them money, and not wanting nothing in return. He did that for a while, until it hit him that he could do that for himself, and take home all the money. Well that's what he started doing. He would go into grocery stores, and ask to speak with the manager. Once the manager would see him and say "Hello", Dusty would kick his script off. He would say "Hello sir/ma'am My wheelchair basketball team is fundraising, to fund our trip to Minnesota, and I was wondering would it be ok if I set up outside your store with my poster board (one that he made up himself of his team playing basketball, and saying fundraiser on it as well), and my candy to sell to your customers if they choose to purchase any?" More often than not he would get the ok on it, and the killer of it is, he would be selling the same type of candy that you could of gotten out of the store for $.50, the same candy we use to sell for $.50 in school, he was selling for $1.00. People would just give him money without taking the candy at times, and on a regular, he would come back home with about $100.00 profit for less than 8 hours work, and to top it off, he use to do it every weekend in different locations, killing them. Sometimes he would do it Saturday, and Sunday depending on how he had things set up.

With the money he would most of the time go buy a new stereo system for his car, or upgrading it, and some more shoes. For a person on the outside looking in, you would of never known how hard he use to grind, and work so many different people, just because they felt sorry for him. He use to go to Swap-O-Rama to get his system for his car, and since he was there so often, he built a little relationship with one of the vendors. He use to say "Hey, I got another amp that I don't like, and was wondering if I can give you that one with some money to upgrade to a better one?" After a little finessing the man, Dusty eventually got him to give in and say that he would do it, that's when he would say "ok, I will be back tomorrow with it, hold this amp here (as he pointed at one) for me", as he left the vendor. Once he got in the car, he would tell Mike "I'm going to clean out one of them blown amps I got, making sure the power light comes on, and trade it with their ass." That's one thing he always did, and that's play on foreigners. He never really cared how they felt because he use to say "they coming over here, and taxing the shit out of us, I'm gonna get mine back, trust that!"

Well the next day, things would go as planned. He would watch the guy hook the amp up making sure the power light came on, and if the guy was about to hook it up to a speaker, he would grab his attention, by asking him all kinds of questions, throwing him off guard. At times when he would hook the amp up, and get no sound due to the amp being blown, he would blame them for messing it up, and start getting loud about how he just bought that amp from them, and that shit don't work, ya'll either did it, fucking it up, or ya'll selling some bullshit as products. After other customers overhearing this, they use to start to circle him listening to what he was saying, questioning the vendors products, or taking Dusty's side, thinking the vendor was trying to take advantage of him being handicapped. He got away with it more often than not. After completing whatever deal he would have made, he would roll back out to the car, pop the trunk, and install the new stereo equipment, before he jumped in the car, then scoot to the drivers seat of the car, breaking his chair down, throwing it in the back seat of his car, and off he would be. He would try and play mike at times, by looking at him after he got in the car, but Mike would just look back! He knew Dusty could handle it himself, but at times he would put it in himself for Dusty.

Not long later Dusty eventually graduated high school and was planning on going off to college. He was accepted into SIUC Southern Illinois University in Carbondale, and was ready for his next step. He was ready to take his show on the road, and hook back up with one of his guys whom he had been playing basketball with since he was a youngster. He was ready to hook up with Earl. Earl had already been going to SIUC, and persuaded Dusty to going there, as well as his cousin Big Stan attended the school.

Chapter 2

Dusty asked Earl "what we drinking on before we hit Beach Bums?", while Earl was ironing his clothes. He always took a long time getting dressed, but it was cool today, Mike was due to arrive by train in a few minutes anyway, so Dusty knew he would have to leave for a minute anyhow to go pick him up! Time kept rolling by and BG stopped through ready to go out as well, and talking shit as usual. That's something they all did every-time they got together. BG was a cool dude. He worked in the dorms Earl and Dusty lived in, and Earl had known him for a while, and introduced them to one another. As they were talking shit, taking turns saying "Earl, you got taco meat on your chest." Or "Earl, why yo leg hanging off your chair like that?, It look like yo foot gangbanging." Before you knew it, Dusty realized what time it was and said "I will be back, I got to go pick up Mike from the train", and headed out. This was what they was waiting to see, because Dusty had told them in advance that Mike was bringing down some car speakers, and amps for him, but they was doubting it, because he rode the train. When the train finally arrived in town, Mike was as happy as a kid in a candy store. He loved the way it looked, and knew that he had an opportunity that a lot of his friends from school aint having. Dusty said "What's up fool? You must like what you see down here" as Mike put his stuff in the car. As the rode off Dusty asked "Did you bring that shit down here?", which Mike said "Yeah" to. The whole ride to Dusty's dorm, Mike was shocked with how many females he saw walking around, and realizing that it wasn't no parents there either. He started thinking to himself "I can get use to this. I might have to make it down here all the damn time."

When they made it to Dusty's room, Mike started unpacking the speakers, when he heard the knocking at the door. It was Earl, and BG! Mike said "what's up" to Earl, because they been known each other, and got introduced to BG as well. While everything got unpacked, Mike gave Dusty a set of 12" subwoofers that he pulled out of his bag, as they were talking about the club for the night. They knew Mike wasn't old enough to get in the club, but before they even started to wonder about him, he told them "go on in the club, I'm just riding, and going to pimp the parking lot." So that's what they did. The next day Dusty came up with another plan, he said "Mike, we about to get you a drivers license, so you can get in the club." He then went on to laying it down how Mike was suppose to do it. He said "I'm going to give you my paperwork, and a wheelchair, so you can go inside the DMV and get you a license", then they left to make that happen. Just like Dusty had expected, it worked like a charm, Mike had his ID, and they were set for the night. The night went off a success.

As time kept moving Dusty felt himself getting sick, so sick that he had to go home because he was having a hard time breathing. When Dusty made it home, and his parents saw how weak his eyes looked, they immediately said "You going to see a doctor in the morning." When the morning came around, Dusty went to the doctor with his mother, and the doctor said "we think it will be best if we hold him for a while, because he has had bronchitis, and it has turned into lung failure." The doctor stated that Dusty has been gasping for breaths, and that's why he been so tired, and sleeping so much. When dusty was admitted into the hospital, the doctors immediately stuck tubes down his throat, and nose to help him breath.

After being in the hospital for about a month, the doctors finally thought they had cured the lung failure, due to him being wide awoke so much, and being active. One day while Mike was sitting there, the doctors came in and spoke to Mike and dusty at the same time saying "guess what? It's your lucky day, we are about to remove the tubes from your mouth and nose today." Mike asked the doctors did they want him to leave the room, which they said "no, you are fine here, it's simple, and we will be real quick. I know he is going to want to talk to you as often as you are here, but his throat is going to be a little soar, so try to let him rest it." As the doctors removed the tubes, Dusty, and Mike were on cloud 9, no more worries. After the tubes were removed, Dusty sat there staring at everyone in the room for a few seconds, then out of nowhere he **flat-lined** in front of every-ones eyes. The doctor yelled "we got an emergency", and rushed mike up out the room, as they started working on him. While Mike was in the hallway, he was crying, and looking for a phone to call his parents on. When he finally found one, he called and said "Ma, Dusty just died." There mother started crying saying "I'm on my way up there!"

A few moments later the doctors came out of the room saying "he is fine, we saved him, but he needs some rest now, but you can go see him for a few minutes." Mike walked in the room full of tears, but trying to stay strong, as he looked at Dusty in the face. Dusty looked back at him as well, and for some strange reason, Mike felt strong. He felt like everything was going to be ok. Dusty gave him that look like he was saying "don't worry, I got this!"

Dusty's parents eventually walked in the room, and had already knew that he was back, because Mike had called them to inform them, but the had other plan's in their mind. They were thinking steps ahead, and had contacted a close family friend to the family, whom was a doctor, and he advised them to get Dusty transferred to the hospital he worked at, because he knew of a specialist there, and he was close with him. He said "if you bring Dusty here, I would be able to get the inside scoop on everything from the doctor, because doctors really don't tell the family all the time the true going ons with their siblings." Well that was enough for them to have made up their mind. That day they scheduled/ had everything set up for Dusty's transfer, and it went through the next day.

After Dusty made it to the next hospital on the west-side of Chicago, they immediately went to tending to him. They started giving him steroids to strengthen his lungs, as well as a bunch of other treatments, which was actually working. Within a months time, Dusty was sent home, but the only problem was that he had to wear an oxygen tank for a while during the day at first, and sleep with a oxygen mask on, to keep something off his lungs. As time kept going by, Dusty kept getting stronger, and winging himself off of the air during the day. Before you knew it, he was back to himself almost. I say maybe 2-3 months went by, and he was off the air completely during the day, and was planning on heading back down to Carbondale to go back to school in the fall. The only difference was that his younger brother Mike was graduating from high school that year, and he would be headed down there as well. So now both of them would be there, easing Dusty's parents mind knowing both their kids would be together, looking after one another.

Unbeknown to Dusty's parents, he never had intentions on taking school serious anymore. He felt like life was to short, and he had been through to much already, so he was aiming for immediate gratification, because his thoughts were that he wasn't going to be around long enough to reap the rewards later in life. One day after Mike graduated from high school Dusty called him over and said "what you plan on doing when you get down there at school?" That had mike kind of stuck, because he had already knew school wasn't for him, his main reason for going was to be near his brother, as well as get away to see something new. Mike sat there and lied with a straight face and said "go to school." Dusty saw right through it, but played like he didn't, but lead to the next thing. He asked "what if I get an apartment off campus, you think you would be with that? That way you won't have to be sharing a shower with other people, and you would be able to smoke without that many worries from the RA's!" Mike didn't give a fuck, he was just trying to get away, so he said "hell yeah I'm with it. I'm really just going there to get the fuck away, get some bread, and watch yo black ass!"

What do you do
When The *Love* You Lost Forever
Comes Back Into Your Life?

GOOD TO
Have You
BACK

a Novel

Toriana Jones

Chapter 1

Gabriella took a nice hot shower and sat down with a bowl of Blue Bell's Banana Pudding ice cream. She felt good about her decision to quit Staten despite not knowing where her new income would come from. She had way too much on her plate to be constantly taking on more and more work without being compensated for it. After Christina found out what was going on she filed for a divorce using her findings as evidence and filed fraud charges against Oscar and Elena. After selling the company to a long time interested party she mailed Gabriella a check that would more than cover the expenses she would have used over the last 4 years, including a vehicle. Christina felt that Gabriella deserved at least half of what she made selling Staten since she was the one to get the company where it was with little or no pay while others reaped the benefits and bogged her down with work. Gabriella had no clue what to do with all the money, at least not right off. She took a few days to make some serious plans about what to do with her life.

She invested a lot of money in stocks and bonds. She purchased a small SUV because she liked the design and didn't have to spend a whole lot of money. She stumbled across a 3 bedroom townhome in foreclosure for less than thirty five thousand. That purchase was made once the inspector determined there was nothing wrong with the property. She made some minor changes, added a few extras before going out to buy furniture to fix the place up. Another thing she decided on was to self-publish her book which would cost a little over eight hundred for the cover, ISBN, bar code and printing for paper and hardback copies to be distributed to local bookstores.

She had been so busy over the last few weeks that Antonio wondered if maybe she was seeing someone else or just tired of him. She hadn't brought the proposal back up or explained what made her cry the way she had the night he proposed. He tried to forget about her. A part of him was saying be patient, she will come around. He had been going back and forth with her for over a year and things just didn't seem to be going anywhere relationship wise.

Gabriella dialed Antonio's number one Friday evening. Hey, how was your day?
Long and tiring he responded. How was yours?
Productive, I was able to accomplish more in one day than I have in years she said with a cheerful voice.
Oh well, that's great. Care to share?
Yes, that's why I called. Was wondering if you would like to go grab a bite to eat tonight. If you don't already have plans maybe come spend the weekend with me she said hopeful. She knew she hadn't been the easiest person to get along with. She had shut him out too many times to count even when he didn't deserve it. Over the past few weeks she had

practically put him on the back burner while she thought things over. Thinking is good, clarity even better but it would be nice to let the people closest to you know what's going on. Cool. I don't have any plans. What time should I pick you up?

I'll pick you up if you don't mind. Unless you just have to drive.

No I'm good. If you want to you can pick me up within 45 minutes to an hour. Gives me time to shower and change.

When she picked Antonio up he was dressed in a brown Christian Audiger shirt that showed off his muscular build along with a pair of blue jeans. He looked good enough to eat. She stepped from her SUV with a smile wearing a khaki slip dress with Coach sandals. Her hair was pulled back into an elegant ponytail. She wrapped her arms around him, inhaled his scent before briefly kissing his cheek. I missed you.

Missed you too woman. What's been up with you lately? You found a boyfriend? He asked these things while still holding on to her and starring into her eyes the way a man looks at a woman he adores.

We have a lot to talk about but no, a boyfriend is not one of them.

You sure? Cause a brother was starting to feel neglected. You been alright though?

Yes, better than ever.

What's this? A rental he asked as he opened the driver's side door she'd gotten out of minutes before.

We have a lot to talk about she repeated.

They decided to have dinner at Ruth Chris. The atmosphere was nice and cozy. Despite the crowd of patrons the service was nice and fast. Before they had the opportunity to dive into conversation their dinner was on the table. Neither of them had bothered with lunch so they both were starved and wasted no time chowing down. Before long their plates were nearly empty.

Sorry Gabriella apologized as she wiped her mouth.

No need, I know how your work load gets pretty busy and you tend to skip lunch.

I take it you did the same thing today?

Haven't had much of an appetite lately.

Why is that?

Because you were on my mind and you have been avoiding me. Why?

She sighed, I haven't been completely honest about my past and I don't know how to tell you all that I've been through.

How about starting with the truth from beginning to end?

Before she could utter another word Ramero stood in front of their table with his cousin Shamar.

Gabi he said with a smile before leaning over to kiss her cheek. It's good to see you.

What's up Shamar asked?

How have you been Ramero asked ignoring the fact that Antonio was sitting there. When Gabriella didn't answer he looked into her eyes with a menacing look. Fine, have it your way. We will talk later. He walked off leaving Gabriella holding her breath as tears threatened to spill from her eyes.

Who was that Antonio asked as he watched Ramero walk away. It wasn't until he was out the door that he focused his attention on Gabriella. His look went to one of concern as he got up and took the seat beside her. Gabi, what's wrong Ma? You gotta talk to me he told her as he wrapped his arms around her.

Ramero's my ex she said as he wiped away her tears.

Okay but that doesn't explain why your reaction is what it is.

Antonio can we just go, please? I don't want to be here anymore. She dropped money to cover their bill plus the tip before getting up from the table and almost hitting the floor. Antonio lifted her up into his arms or at least planned to when she argued that she was okay. He put an arm around her shoulder and told her At least let me drive. She passed him the keys. Instead of driving to her place he drove to his. He picked a sleeping Gabriella up in his arms and carried her inside. He lit candles inside his bathroom, turned on the music, started a hot bubble bath using Eucalyptus Peppermint Body Wash from Bath & Body Works. He undressed her, lifted her up into his arms again and placed her in the awaiting bath. He bathed her as if you would a newborn baby without starring or making her uncomfortable. Afterwards he dried her off, placed her in bed, removed everything except his boxers and got into bed pulling her onto his chest where she slept peacefully in his arms for the first time in years.

Antonio's house phone is what awakened them the next morning. His brother Adam was at his front door to borrow money. Aside from the ringing phone his constant beating on the door caused Gabriella to jump.

What's going on she asked in alarm?

Antonio kissed her forehead, Calm down Gabi. It's just Adam he said as he searched her face. He came to borrow money. You okay?

She threw herself back on the bed pulling another pillow over her head as she screamed into it.

Antonio left the room to answer the front door after closing the bedroom door behind him. He hoped to make Adam's visit quick so he could get back to Gabriella. Adam made his way inside and asked You got any breakfast food man? I'm starved.

Some cereal, there's some turkey bacon and sausage in there too. If you cook make enough for me and...

Gabi's here?

Yeah. Make yourself at home he said as he turned to leave the room.

Gabriella was awake and dressed in yesterday's clothes. What are you doing Antonio asked?

I'm about to go home and...

And what? Yeah right, you're not going anywhere.

I need to change clothes.

He opened a drawer, pulled out a t-shirt and a pair of sweats that he passed to her. Here, put these on.

She starred at him. He starred back. Adam's making breakfast. We're supposed to be spending the weekend together, remember? You're not going anywhere without me until Sunday night, if I let you out of my sight then.

She smiled for the first time since Ramero showed up at the restaurant. Antonio after breakfast I need to go to my place to…

I'm going with you. He walked into the bathroom, passed her a toothbrush and a face towel. He stood beside her at the sink where they both brushed their teeth and washed their faces. We're going to have our conversation about last night before this day is over with.

Yes sir.

Gabi, I'm serious.

Okay. Ramero's my ex and he's also the reason I don't trust anyone.

You don't trust me? Well I guess that's obvious because if you did you would have told me all this long ago.

She turned to look into his eyes but he started out of the bathroom. She grabbed his hand, he snatched it away and kept walking.

Antonio, I do trust you she said barely above a whisper. If I didn't I wouldn't be here right now.

Why do you keep me at arm's length? You tell me just enough to shut me up. Gabi that's not enough for me.

What do you want to know?

I want to know everything, the good, the bad and the ugly.

Antonio I have a horrible past.

He saw the pain, the tears, the worry. He pulled her into his arms. Gabi, nothing can be that bad.

Adam stuck around a couple of hours after breakfast enjoying his brother and Gabi's company.

You ready Antonio asked her?

Yeah, I have some confessions to make.

You're cheating on me?

No she laughed.

You're pregnant?

God no, I would have to have sex to get pregnant and…

You used to be a man?

Shut up she laughed as she playfully pushed him.

So what is it man?

I quit my job.

Cool he said calmly knowing how her job stressed and depressed her at the same time. You find something else?

No. I've decided to self publish my book she said waiting to hear the negativity she was sure to come.

Congratulations he told her as he picked her up in his arms twirling her around on the sidewalk while kissing her cheeks. You need help with anything?

Smiling she said No, I'm good. Thanks

When did you do all this?

A few weeks ago.

Oh yeah, we keeping secrets now he asked never letting her feet touch the ground.

Not intentionally, I just didn't know how you would take it that's all.

Do me a favor.

What's that?

Stop worrying about how I'm going to respond to things and just tell me what's on your mind.

I moved.

Where to?

Madison Gardens

Whoa, did you get a contract already?

She laughed again, No. The day I quit my job was the last time you and I went out for lunch. I had another annual review with no raise, no mention of a promotion, only more work added to my job description. I couldn't take it anymore.

That's understandable, the job was stressing you out and it wasn't paying enough. I would have done the same thing…

But what?

I don't understand why you would move into such an expensive community without having a job. Now that I don't understand.

The day I quit I had a talk with Mrs. Bradford. She was not pleased with my leaving the company. She was convinced that she had compensated me enough to where I would never leave the company. Had I been given the many benefits she had outlined in her proposal for me 4 years ago I probably never would have.

I don't understand.

4 years ago Christina promoted me to VP over accounting, gave me $35 an hour, a company paid vehicle of my choice, all paid living expenses, a company credit card in which I could use for whatever and an ass load of other amenities.

What?

Elena, my boss, she never presented the proposal to me. Instead she kept feeding me bullshit about how they couldn't give me a raise or a promotion. Meanwhile her and Christina's husband had made a new life living off what was supposed to be my salary. The company car, Elena drove. The condo, she and Oscar lived in when Christina was away on business which was often enough. They even used the company credit card to shop, take trips and do a number of other things while passing everything off as my expenses. If Christina had not shown up the day I quit I would have never known. I could have been sued for all that money.

Damn.

I know right?

So did they pay you back for the 4 years you weren't being paid?

Yes, all that and then some.

That's what's up.

Chapter 2

So, Ramero, was he your first love?
Yes she sighed, I once thought he was my everything.
And then what happened?
He used me and dropped me like a pile of garbage. Basically he left me to die.
How so?
He got caught up in a federal drug case. To shorten his sentence he started snitching on people. He made them think it was me. Not only was he trying to put all his charges on me and set me up as the ring leader he also wanted everyone on the outside to think I was the one snitching so he could get off scott-free. He even went so far as to allow two men to rape me to prove that I deserved what was coming to me and that he had nothing to do with it.
Were you really raped?
Yes she sighed but that's not the end of it. He owed one guy a half million dollars, he told the guy I ran off with his money. He made me his sex slave for over a year. He at first held me against my will, threatened me with guns, beatings, death. He had infant children that he would leave with me and his bodyguards from time to time. His kids fell in love with me, as did he. But because of what he'd done to me in the past I could never love him. He finally gave me the opportunity to tell him what really happened. He hated himself for it.
Antonio stood there stunned. Damn Gabi, no wonder you won't let me touch you.
She sighed, I've been going to counseling. I'm getting help talking out my problems, my past mistakes and I'm desperately trying to move on with my life. I was once told I would never amount to anything and that I would be dead before I turned 21. Well I'm about to be 25 and I'm still alive so I figured its' time to start living. I go to counseling three times a week. I hope you understand why I'm not so easily trusting of everyone. I've been through far more than what I've shared with you today. If I could, I would tell you more but its' too painful and too much for me to talk about in one setting. For someone that cares about me I'm sure it's even harder for them to hear it.

Ramero showed up at Images the salon Gabriella had been going to since she was in the 9th grade. He waited for her to walk out of the salon. She wore her hair in loose curls, face free of makeup rocking an electric blue sundress by Bebe with a pair of sandals on her pretty pedicured feet. She was still just as beautiful as the day he met her at a track meet when she was in the 7th grade.
Juicy he called out to her, stopping her in her tracks as she walked ahead of him. Slow up, I just want to talk to you for a minute.
You and I have nothing to talk about.
But we do, look he pleaded. I want to apologize for all the things I did and said to you. I know right now that don't mean shit, probably never will but I needed to say it to you.
Thank you Ramero she said as she started walking again without turning around.

Satin told me something when I came home and I need to know if it's true. Again she stopped. Gabi, please.

Yes it's true. I was pregnant with your baby but he died while I was giving birth and I almost died too after being beaten for 72 hours by men that thought I was trying to put them away for life with stories I couldn't have possibly told because I never knew. She gave that time to sink in before saying Ramero, that's not the first child we lost. Your daughter managed to breathe for 2 whole hours before she died from a gunshot wound to her chest when you shot me in the stomach. She wiped away tears and sighed, is there anything else you want to know before I walk away one last time?

Whatever happened with you and Tech?

He fucked me for over a year before he fell in love with me and gave me back my freedom. Were you ever pregnant by him?

Yes but you made sure I lost that one too when you set me up to be kidnapped, beaten because you heard I was no longer being tortured but cared for by the man you despised. You know Tech is dead right?

Got a phone call this morning. He died of heart failure they say.

A broken heart is what I heard because he never stopped loving you. You going to his funeral?

Yeah I will be there.

She had to convince Antonio that she would be okay traveling to New York alone to attend Tago "Tech" Diaz's funeral.

When she arrived in New York Tech's brother Drago picked her up from the airport and greeted her with a welcoming hug and cheek kisses.

Good to see you Bella, only I wish it were under better circumstances.

You and me both. How have you been? How are Isabella and Fernando holding up?

The whole family is distraught, it's chaotic. I honestly don't know what to do.

With what?

With everything he said sadly. Tech was the one that held this all together.

Yeah, he was damn good at it too Gabriella said with a sad smile.

Can I ask you a question?

Sure, go ahead.

Did you ever love my brother?

Gabriella turned the radio down, lost her smile as her eyes glazed over with tears. I loved him but I hated him at the same time.

Why?

Did he ever tell you how we hooked up?

He said he won a bet but over the years talking about you made him sad and I always thought there was more to the story.

*There is or at least there was but Drago I'm not quite sure this conversation is fit for the day.
I don't think you could handle it on top of everything else that's going on.*

*Speak for yourself Bella, I'm a man. Trust me, I can handle it. Now if it's too much for you I
can understand.*

Do you really want to know?

*Yes I want to know how you could walk away from the man that worshiped the ground you
walked on and gave you the world.*

Drago do you remember the way it was when you first came to live with Tago?

Yes he taught me everything.

Between me and Tago I mean, do you remember?

Yes, it was as if you hated him. The two of you would always argue and fight.

*Your brother never put his hands on me, at least not in that way. I was brought to Tago's
against my will. I was there to pay off a debt and for a whole year I was your brother's whore
so to speak.*

*What? Yeah right. I don't believe this shit. How dare you use my brother's name in vain?
That man loved you.*

In the end he did but in the beginning I was just his pussy.

But why? What did you owe him?

*I didn't owe him anything. My ex- boyfriend and him were in business together. My ex got
locked up and did away with half a million of your brother's money. The Feds took over the
case so my ex started singing like a canary. When word got out that someone was snitching
he wanted to take the blame off himself so he somehow convinced everyone involved that I
was doing the talking. He also convinced Tago that I ran off with his money. Tago never
believed I was guilty of snitching but he did believe I took his money. So for one year he
made me work off his money by having sex with him. She laughed sadly, I never could
understand it all. Had I met Tago before all this and been single I'd have fucked him without
a thought. I tried to explain this to him on many occasions but he never believed me. He
trusted Ramero just that much.*

Ramero?

Yes, he was my ex.

*Get the fuck out of here. When my brother said he was in love with Ramero's girl he was
talking about you? I thought that was what the two of you fought about all the time, him
messing around with other women.*

When Tago got serious about me it scared him. There were no other women at that point.

So how did he ever find out the truth?

*By the time he did I was already pregnant with his child and he wanted to keep it. I wanted
to keep her too. I had even planned to settle down with Tago despite all that happened but
then I went out shopping one day. Ramero and his boys kidnapped me. They beat me and
tortured me until I lost the baby. Ramero was okay with me working off his debt as Tago's
whore but he couldn't stomach Tago and I being together in that sense. While Tago*

searched for me they went through my things back at the house. I kept a notebook, I wrote down everything that had happened from the time all this mess with Ramero started. Tago read it and he finally realized I had been telling the truth all along.

Man, I don't believe this shit. My brother could have had any woman he wanted. Why would he need you to have sex with him to pay off a debt?

That's the part I never understood.

And Ramero where is he now?

He's supposed to be at the funeral. He made it a point to let me know that.

Does my brother know he did this to you?

No, I never told him because I didn't want him to do something stupid and end up in prison. The Feds were all over him but couldn't make the charges stick. I knew if he even made a threat he would be gone. I didn't want that to happen.

So how did you leave?

After a while what Tago did to me started to bother him and he let me go.

You know my brother never got over you leaving right?

So I've heard. I really wish things could have been different. In another life I'd have married your brother and gave him everything but I had so much taken away from me during all that. I just couldn't take anymore so I walked away. I had to.

Whatever happened with Ramero? How did he get out? He was just as big in this as my brother. And if he was snitching, why ain't nobody after him now?

Last I heard there was a confidential informant working the case and they granted him immunity because he was also involved with more than one undercover agent on an intimate level.

www.ingramcontent.com/pod-product-compliance
Lightning Source LLC
Chambersburg PA
CBHW051244170626
46809CB00004B/1482